About the author

Born in Toronto, Shirley Fa lost her mother at a young and grew up with her fat stepmother, brother and sist in a small flat above a synagogue on Bellevue Avenue. While still a teenager, she married and had a daughter, but the marriage fell apart. She traveled extensively throughout the United States and Europe and worked for a while at the *Daily Herald* in London. To enhance her grade eight education, she read voraciously: Flannery O'Connor, Chekhov, Malamud—and later Mavis Gallant, Margaret Laurence and Alice Munro, each of whom would become a friend and admirer.

For many years she presided over a theatrical rooming house on Sherbourne Street, holding court at its famous kitchen table and telling tales of Yankev the Bootlegger, Henye the Hunchback, Motele the Blabbermouth and Raisel the Galloping Consumptive. It was her third husband, actor-director James Edmond, who finally sent the actors and ballerinas packing—and sent Shirley upstairs to write down the stories she had honed in their midst.

She made her literary debut at the age of sixty with a story in the *Atlantic Monthly* in 1967 and over the next decade or so published eight more stories in prominent magazines. In 1979 she published *Everything In The Window*, which the *New Yorker* called "a striking first novel." In 1988 McClelland & Stewart published her collected stories as *A Basket of Apples and Other Stories*. Although Faessler died in 1997, the present volume—containing all six of her acclaimed "Kensington Market" stories—brings her splendid literary voice back to vivid life.

A Basket of Apples

Stories by Shirley Faessler

Now and Then Books
Toronto 2014

Publisher's website:
www.nowandthenbookstoronto.com

ISBN 978-0-9919009-2-3

The publisher would like to thank Karen L. Hines, the author's
granddaughter, for kindly allowing us to publish these stories
and for her enthusiastic support of and assistance with this
project. The publisher is also grateful to Lily Poritz Miller for
contributing the Foreword. Thanks also to Chris Cran, Miriam
Beckerman, Jeannine Locke and Bena Shuster.

Library and Archives Canada Cataloguing in Publication

Faessler, Shirley, author
    A basket of apples : stories / by Shirley Faessler.

ISBN 978-0-9919009-2-3 (pbk.)
    I. Title.

PS8561.A37B3 2014   C813'.54   C2014-901227-6

Contents

Foreword: Remembering Shirley

I FIRST MET SHIRLEY FAESSLER in the early 1970s. I was a newcomer to Canada and had been brought to Toronto by Jack McClelland to join his company as senior editor. Canada was in need of experienced editors at that time and I had honed my skills by working in New York for about a decade. It was my role to work with established writers but also to develop the fountain of burgeoning talent in the country.

One day Jack McClelland ran into my office and said, "I want you to go over to this house on Sherbourne Street and meet a lady who has been struggling with a manuscript for years. She's ready to burn the pages."

When I clanked up the wooden steps of the old house near Wellesley and rang the bell, there was a long silence. I looked around the dreary street and wondered if I was at the right place. Finally, the heavy, glass-paned door opened and there stood a tiny figure in a house dress. Her huge soulful eyes swept over me with suspicion. "Are you the editor?"

Pattering in slippers, she led me into the kitchen dominated by a long wooden table. The walls of the room and the refrigerator were covered with photos of beautiful smiling people. Who were these people? I wondered. I was later to learn that this had been a rooming house for actors.

The kettle whistled and she put a mug of tea before me. She sat down and set her blazing eyes on me. "So you're an editor?" she asked with a touch of irony. "What is an editor supposed to do?"

I fumbled that it was to help an author express himself.

"So you're going to take my manuscript and put it into good English?"

I denied that, not sure why I was really there.

"*My* people don't talk good English."

"That's fine."

"Jack McClelland said you were going to help me. Maybe you'll help me burn the whole thing. It's been a nightmare trying to write this novel."

Jack had discovered Shirley when he read her stories in the *Atlantic Monthly*, *Saturday Night* and *Tamarack Review*. Though the world of the Jewish immigrants in the Kensington Market area of Toronto in the 1920s and 1930s was alien to this Anglo-Saxon man who had been educated at Upper Canada College and the University of Toronto, he was intrigued by the world Shirley recreated and recognized a unique talent. He was also captivated by this miniature lady who had not gone beyond grade eight and reigned in her kitchen like an empress. His other authors expected to be indulged at the Inn on the Park or the elegant restaurants in downtown Toronto, but Shirley received her guests only in her kitchen. Through her stories she had won the admiration of Margaret Laurence, Adele Wiseman, Mavis Gallant and Alice Munro, and several literary critics also visited her kitchen.

Publishing a book of short stories at that time was as bleak a prospect as poetry. No one would read it. Jack wanted Shirley to reach a wider audience and he had urged her to write a novel. Though she would patter up the stairs to the little room where she had an old typewriter, she would stare at the blank pages or else rip up whatever she produced. Her stories had encompassed an entire world within a few pages and now she was supposed to extend it to several hundred.

The pressure of having an editor arrive in her kitchen didn't hasten the process. She seemed to freeze. Though I tried to phone her a few times, I soon realized I had become her enemy. So I stayed away.

I was surprised when one day a few months later I received a call from her.

"I guess you've given up on me altogether," she declared.

I recognized the voice. "Oh, Shirley, how are *you*?" I didn't dare ask how her writing was going.

"You're supposed to be this great editor from New York. Am I ever going to see you again?"

There was no formality with Shirley and I went over to her house that evening. It was then that I met the tall blond elegant man who had been her partner for many years.

"James Edmond," she announced. "Does he look like an actor to you?"

James had been one of the aspiring actors who lived in her rooming house. He was born into an Anglo-Saxon family in a small Ontario town and this strange little lady intrigued him. James had a love of literature and they would read together from Chekhov in the morning. As a young girl Shirley had fallen for a blond athletic coach who became the father of her daughter, and she had an eye for the fair-haired young men who emerged from a world unlike her own. Though Shirley was considerably older than James, they became life partners.

By the time I met Shirley she was elderly. Her age was a mystery. On the one hand she was a mischievous child, performing wicked tricks; and yet she seemed ancient, the huge eyes containing a world one longed to enter. She once said, "I'm the oldest person I know."

Though Shirley and I became friends and I spent many evenings with her, I had to remind myself why I was in her life. I was supposed to help bring her novel to fruition. Yet I knew I had to tread easily, that pressure would only cause her to freeze and become suspicious of me again. She had little regard for editors, and her friends Adele Wiseman and Margaret Laurence shared her feelings. They were fearful of editors who had an inclination to rewrite an author's work and tamper with the language.

Miraculously and secretly the pages in Shirley's manuscript seemed to grow, and it was now that she would be calling me. "Lily Poritz Miller," she would announce. "How did you ever happen to get such a long name? Is that because you're an editor?"

I would try to deny I was an editor.

When I finally received the heap of pages and dragged them home, I was afraid to read them. She had spent almost a decade struggling with them and when she gave the manuscript to me she said, "If you decide to burn it, I won't be mad. Just take it away from me."

I had to be careful because this was in the 1970s, before the computer, and the copy she gave me was the only one in existence. I also had to be cautious about the comments I dared to make. Could this backfire and cause Shirley to be blocked forever as a writer?

I tread on my toes, never used a pen which suggested permanence, made my comments in light pencil, always as a query rather than a statement. I was nervous when I handed the pages back to her. I knew she conferred with James, who seemed supportive of me. He was a lovely, witty man who had endured Shirley's struggle with the manuscript, and he longed to see it come to light. And so the novel, *Everything in the Window*, was finally published in 1979. The reviews were mixed; and though Shirley would continue to patter upstairs to her typewriter, I never saw anything new.

The pressures of the publishing world consumed me and for some years I lost touch with Shirley. But occasionally she would phone and I'd go to her kitchen for tea and talk. She spoke often of her past, of the fair-haired athletic coach who had become the father of her daughter, but even more about her second husband who seemed to have been a devilish character and had amassed a fair amount of money through questionable means. She appeared to admire his illicit tactics and spoke of him with humour and irony.

The 1980s were moving on and time seemed to mellow Shirley. I kept thinking of the treasure of her stories that were fading into obscurity. I began to gather them and reread them, and I felt these should not be lost to the world. Though several had been published in the *Atlantic Monthly*, *Best American Short Stories*, *Saturday Night* and *Tamarack Review*, and were broadcast on the CBC, I felt they should be contained in a book that would have a longer life. And so I began to retread my steps to the old house on Sherbourne Street and sit in the kitchen with Shirley and James. The collection was published in 1988 as *A Basket of Apples and Other Stories*, and received unanimous praise.

Shirley Faessler died in 1997. A garden was created in her memory in the Huron Street Gardens behind the

Lillian H. Smith Library at College and Spadina. The plaque, designed by James Edmond, Shirley's companion of forty years, read: "This lily garden is planted in memory of Shirley Faessler by those who loved her. In her life and her writing, she celebrated this area's Jewish past." The garden was lovingly tended by James and later by her daughter Bernice and others. But sadly, while the garden continues to bloom, Shirley's written legacy has fallen into obscurity.

In May 2013 I attended the launch of a book that immortalized the old Jewish community in Toronto— *Only Yesterday: Collected Pieces on the Jews of Toronto* by Ben Kayfetz and Stephen Speisman, published by Now and Then Books of Toronto. As I listened to the impassioned words of publisher Bill Gladstone, Shirley Faessler's stories sprang back to my mind. It was twenty-five years since the book had been published in 1988. I felt I should share the stories with the publisher. I was delighted when he informed me that he would bring the book back to life so that Shirley and the Yiddish-speaking immigrants of the Kensington Market area of Toronto in the 1920s and 1930s would not be forgotten. — *Lily Poritz Miller*

The Stories

For my sister, Gertie

and my brother, Louis

Henye

FRIDAYS AFTER SCHOOL I used to get a nickel from Henye for going with her to the Grace Street Hospital to speak English for her. I was ten years old and it was a terrible embarrassment for me to be seen on the street with her, she was so ugly.

Henye was a skinny little woman, all bone, no flesh to her. Her hair, which she wore in two braids around her head, was the same colour as her skin, pallid. Her nose was long, her voice was hoarse, and on top of everything else she was bent over in the back.

She would hang on to my arm all the way to the clinic, pinching it now and then when she felt my attention was wandering from the recap she was giving me of her ailments, things to tell the doctor. We would take our place on the bench, Henye hunched forward with feet dangling free of the floor, her black stockings twisted and spiralled at the spindle-leg ankles, and wait for our number to be called. Our turn would come and I would give the doctor a rundown of her troubles, she all the while prompting me in Yiddish: "*Zog im, Soreh, zog im.*" She wanted me to tell him she had not moved her bowels in three days. I

15

would sooner have died. "I told him!" I would say to her in English. It was bad enough I was obliged to acknowledge before the Gentile doctor that I understood the Yiddish she was speaking, let alone speak it in front of him. Before the nickel was yielded up to me I would have to accompany her back to her house, even though she knew the way home. Not till we were in the house did she take from her pocket the knotted handkerchief in which she kept her change. Her husband, Yankev, who was my stepmother's uncle, would be home from his day's business when I returned his wife from the Outpatients. (Being Friday, Yankev saw to it that the day's business which consisted mainly of deliveries—he was a bootlegger—was done with and finished before *Erev Shabbus*.) "Well?" he would say to me as Henye was unknotting the handkerchief. "Did she get a little pinch from the doctor? A tickle, a little feel? She likes that, the old devil."

Yankev, at that time in his late fifties, was a tall, thickset, handsome man with a bushy head of hair beginning to grey. He was a vigorous, illiterate, coarse-natured man with a ribald sense of humour. He loved a bit of mischief, a practical joke. Henye, a year younger than her husband but who looked old enough to be his mother, was a sobersides. Yankev and Henye made a striking pair; the contrast between husband and wife was something to see.

Yankev had a twin. His brother Yudah, whom (it was said) Yankev loved more than he did his own children. The twin brothers, Yankev and Yudah, were identical. In build, in countenance and voice they were one and the same. I never learned to tell them apart, nor could neighbours or friends distinguish between them. But my stepmother, who was their niece, could tell one from the other. And so could my father, who had no use for either of them . . . .

My mother died when my brother, my sister and I were very young; and a year or so after her death, my father, in search of a wife to make a home for his motherless children, met through the offices of a matchmaker the brothers Yankev and Yudah, who were seeking a husband for their niece Chayele, whom they had brought over from the old country. The brothers, after the meeting took place, were not too keen on the match. They thought my father, a Rumanian immigrant who could speak English and could read and write, gave himself too many airs—for a poor man. On the other hand, here was Chayele, an old maid of thirty-five and altogether without prospects, so they gave in. But they never took to my father. Nor did he to my stepmother's family of Russian immigrants.

Yankev and Yudah were born in Chileshea, a village somewhere in the depths of Russia, Yankev the older of the pair by fifteen minutes. When the time came, they were married to wives picked for them by their father. Yankev, in his twenty-first year and older than his brother by fifteen minutes, was the first to be betrothed. The father's choice for Yankev fell to the daughter of a landowner in Propoiske, a village a few miles from theirs. Yankev was informed by his father of the business and a week later he set out with his father by horse and cart for the seven-mile journey to Propoiske to meet his wife-to-be, Henye.

17

The following, as was told (again and again) by Yankev himself, is an account of the meeting:

There was a bitter frost that night. It was black as pitch when we started out, not even a dog was to be seen on the road. We came to my beloved's house cold as stones. The landowner opened the door to us and we were conducted to a big room with a round table in it, a davenport, a carpet on the floor—very fine. He invited me to the stove to warm myself, giving me several glances. Then to my father he gave a nod. Satisfied.

Satisfied. Why would he not be satisfied? Warming himself at the stove stood a stunning youth—you should have seen me at twenty-one, I was like a tree. Tall, straight, a head of hair like a lion, a neck like a bull. He took a few steps to the hall, my future father-in-law, and called for his wife. Right away a scrap of a woman came hurrying in. So fast I thought she was on wheels. A nothing of a woman, the size of a sitting dog. She gave me a dried hand, looking me up and down.

"Well, mamushka," her husband said to her, "are you pleased with your future son-in-law?"

Her voice, when it came out, was a croak. "It is not for me to say. It's for Henyechke to say. If she is pleased with him, I will be content."

A second time the landowner went to the hall. "Come, Henyechke," he called to his daughter. "We're waiting for you."

The door opened and my beloved came to the room. One look and everything went black before my eyes. A duplicate of the mother! A chill fell on me. One minute I was cold, the next minute hot. She gave me her hand. "Welcome to our house," she said. The voice even was like the mother's. We were bidden to table and my sweetheart pouring out the tea did not take her eyes from me. Devouring me with her eyes.

Meantime, the mother—and this is something you would have to see with your own eyes to believe—was doling out the sugar. Breaking it off piece by piece from the sugar bowl which she kept in her lap between a pair of bony knees.

Heed yourself, Yankev, an inner voice warned me. Heed yourself.

We drank a second glass of tea, we ate a stingy piece of cake, a spoonful of cherry jam, and it was time to go. My father took my hand and placed it in the hand of my future bride, and the pact was made. Unhappy, ill-fated Yankev was now betrothed. It seemed to me I heard a howling of wolves. That witches were coupling, I knew for sure.

I whipped up the horse and we started for home. He talked and he talked and he talked, my father, so pleased was he with this night's business. The handsome dowry he had negotiated for his son, pitting his wits against the landowner's. I would not have to work like a horse to earn a bitter piece of bread as he at my age had done. I could go into business, or buy a piece of land. In a year or I would be looked up to, respected. He kept on and on. Words piling up, every one of them a stone in my heart. The business of the dowry had not been as easy as I might think, he told me. I was not the only suitor. There was another candidate.

"Who?" I said, speaking for the first time. "The Devil?"

"Enough, Yankev!" he hollered. "Enough!"

We were late getting home. My mother had gone to her bed, but not my brother Yudah to his. He was waiting to hear my news, I had left with such high hopes. I was a lusty youth at twenty-one—vital! One look at my face and he did not have to ask how I had fared. He signed to me behind my father's back and I followed him to the room we slept in together. I fell on his neck and poured out to him my bitter

19

heart. He rocked me in his arms and hushed me like a baby. "Shah, shah, shah." He bade me to compose myself. He had a plan.

"Tomorrow in a quiet moment I will propose it to my father," he said.

What plan? I tried to worry it out of him but all I could get from him was, "Rest easy, Yankev. Leave everything to me."

And as a condemned man with his head already in the noose clings foolishly to the hope of a reprieve, I was calmed by his words.

His plan? I heard it next morning. Keeping myself out of sight behind the kitchen door I heard the plan as he put it to my father.

"I beg you, Father, let me stand in my brother's place under the canopy. No one can tell us apart. Even you and my mother sometimes have to take a second look to make sure." (True. The pranks we had played on *shiksas* in the fields—and even on respectable Jewish girls in our village!)

"Who put you up to this?" my father asked him. "Your brother?"

"On my word, my brother knows nothing of this plan."

"Why do you do it then?"

My brother returned no answer.

I jumped from my hiding place. "For pity!" I shouted. "For pity, do you hear!"

My father lifted his hand as if to strike me. Which I deserved, raising my voice to my father.

"There will be no trickery," he said. "I gave my hand to the landowner, and Yankev gave his hand to the daughter . . . ."

In a month's time Yankev and Henye were man and wife.

The first child of the marriage, a boy, was born sickly.

He lived only two weeks. The second child, again a boy, was a compact, healthy child. He sickened and in six weeks was dead.

Henye, brooding, mourning the loss of her children, took a strange notion into her head. Two children one after the other had been snatched from her. A punishment, surely. A judgement. She had sinned, wronged, and was now being repaid . . . .

The night of the betrothal when Yankev's father on the way home from Propoiske told his son there was another candidate for the hand of the landowner's daughter, he was speaking the truth. Not the Devil, as Yankev conjectured, but a young man from Samatevitz who, prior to Yankev by a week or two, had been viewed and sent on his way after tea, a piece of cake and cherry jam, with a half-promise (which he took to be a firm commitment) that the dowry together with the landowner's daughter was as good as his. A week or two later, when Henye clapped eyes on Yankev, all was up with the suitor from Samatevitz. The jilted suitor made a fuss. He demanded compensation. In rubles. The landowner peaced him off with soft words. The rejected suitor left in a dudgeon, making an ominous pronouncement. "God will repay me," he said.

God will repay me—

These words came back to Henye, chilling her heart. Pregnant again and determined not to let this one slip away from her, she conceived a plan for holding on to her third child. To ensure the continuance of the child about to be born to her, she must solicit the pardon of her rejected lover.

21

She was resolved that unless she petitioned his forgiveness, no issue of hers would live to see the light of day.

Her third son was born and Henye, to ward off the Evil Eye, gave him the name Alter (Old One). Then as soon after the birth as she was able to, she put her plan into operation. She clothed the infant in old swaddling clothes, tatters, and journeyed with him by foot to the cemetery where her rejected suitor (who in the interim had died) lay buried. There, by his grave, she pleaded for pardon. Holding in her arms a ragamuffin whom no one on earth, or under, could conceivably covet, she begged forgiveness for the wrong she had done him.

Alter survived and thrived. At sixteen he was almost as tall as his father, Yankev. Five more were born after him. The last born of the five, a girl. All persevered and held fast. Henye became shrunken and humped over in the back.

Yudah too had married and was fathering a family.

A few months after Yankev's marriage to Henye, the father negotiated for Yudah a marriage with a girl called Lippa, a pretty girl from a nearby village. Yudah, as was the custom, brought his wife home after the marriage, and lodged her under the parental roof. With Lippa, the family consisted of seven. The old people, the twins, their wives, and Chayele, orphaned grandchild of the old people. (The child's mother, sister of the twins and older by a few years, was widowed early in marriage and died shortly after, leaving Chayele orphaned.)

Over the years Lippa gave birth to four children; the firstborn a boy, and the other three, girls.

THE OLD PEOPLE DIED and the twin brothers in their forty-third year decided to emigrate to the new world. Yankev taking with him Alter, and Yudah taking his firstborn, the brothers set out, their wives and remaining children to be sent for when they were settled. They set sail for the new world, all four, not a word of English among them. Their language was Yiddish. To their work people and to the peasants in the field they spoke Russian. Not one had been a greater distance than fifty miles (if that) from Chileshea. They brought food on board ship, not knowing for sure if they would be fed. They docked in Halifax, thinking they were in America.

They entrained for Toronto and were met at the station by a gang of people: *landsmen*, relatives, a junto of compatriots who had emigrated years before. The first few weeks were given over entirely to conviviality. Parties were given for them, dinners, suppers; days and nights were spent in nostalgic reminiscence. Their cousin Haskele (called behind his back Haskele the Shikker) toured the twins with their sons around the city in his car. He showed them Eaton's, Simpsons, the City Hall, Sunnyside, the Parliament buildings, Casa Loma, the Jewish market on Kensington and the McCaul Street synagogue.

Finally the business at hand—how to make a living—came up for consideration. The brothers were counselled, warned what to watch out for. Toronto was not Chileshea. Plenty of crooks on the lookout for a pair of greenhorns with money in their pocket. It was decided after a succession of councils and advisement that the best plan would be to start small. The name Chaim the Schnorrer (gone to his rest a few months since) came up at one of these sessions. He had started small and was rich as Croesus when he died. His investment? A few dollars for a peddler's licence, a few dollars for a pushcart—and the wealth he accumulated in six years!

Who knew how rich he was getting, the fish-peddling miser. He lived in a garret and slept on two chairs put together and ate dreck. We took pity on him. Only when he was dying in the Western Hospital from dried-up guts that it came out how much money he had. He grabbed a hold of every doctor who put a nose even in the public ward and begged them to save him. "Save me," he told them. "I've got money, I can pay." He showed them bankbooks. A thousand in this bank, two thousand in another bank. In his shoes alone they found four hundred dollars.

The brothers obtained a fish-peddling licence each, equipped themselves with carts, and taking over Chaim the Schnorrer's circuit peddled their fish in the Jewish district, the area bounded by College and Spadina, Dundas and Bathurst streets, and beyond. And made a good thing of it. In less than three years they were able to provide passage for their families.

Henye arrived with their four sons, their daughter and their niece Chayele. Yudah, his wife Lippa having died a year after his departure, had only his three daughters to greet.

All this happened years before I was born . . . .

When Chayele came to us as stepmother I was six years old. We lived in rooms over the synagogue on Bellevue Avenue; and Yankev with his wife, Henye, and their daughter, Malke, who was a dipper at Willard's Chocolates and engaged to be married to a druggist, lived around the corner from us on Augusta Avenue. Their youngest son, Pesach, lived with his wife, Lily, in the upstairs flat of his father's house. Their other four sons were domiciled with their wives and children around and about the city.

Yudah lived with a married daughter a few blocks from his brother's place.

Yankev was a social man. He loved company and almost every night of the week friends and relatives would gather at his house on Augusta Avenue. My stepmother too went there almost every night, and I used to tag along with her. I loved going to Yankev's, what a hullabaloo! No one spoke, everyone shouted, Yankev's voice rising above the hurly-burly.

"Henye!" he would call out when the full number was assembled. "Where is she, my beauty?"

Henye would be sitting in a corner of the kitchen apart from the hubbub; and Yankev, who knew exactly where she was located, would make a great play of searching her out. Looking to the right of him, to the left of him, behind him, he would lift his head finally and craning it over the assembled company would direct his glance to her station.

"Ah, there she is, my picture. What are you sitting there

like a stump? People are in the house. Bring something to table. Fruit, a piece of cake. Make tea."

Henye would rise to fill the kettle, while Yankev, his eye on her, might mutter sotto voce: "Crooked Back."

Night after night they sat at Henye's table, friends and relatives, eating her food and laughing at Yankev's abuse of her. Now and then, not out of loyalty to her or compassion, but for the sake of mischief, for the sake of quickening the action, Henye would be prodded by one of the company to defend herself, to make some reply to her husband. "Say something to him, Henye!"

Hunched over in a corner chair and blowing on her tea which she drank from a saucer, Henye would lift her shoulder in a shrug. "Let him talk," she would say, making her standard reply, her voice grating, harsh. "As a dog howls so Yankev speaks. Does one dispute with a howling dog? Let him talk."

One time I saw her go into a frenzied tantrum at Yankev's Crooked-Back remark. Crooked Back was a commonplace in his vocabulary of insults. He had worse names for her. Old Devil, Witch, Scarecrow—these names went unheeded by Henye, were passed over with a shrug from her, a spit on the floor. But this night for some unanswerable reason she was stung, inflamed by Yankev's "Crooked Back" as she was filling the kettle. She went berserk. She stamped her feet like Rumpelstiltskin. Slammed the kettle, spilling water from the spout. With head thrust forward and bony arms bent at the elbow, she busied herself with the back of her dress, unfastening it at the neck. Pulling at her undergarments till she had them far down enough to expose and lay bare her disfigurement, she turned her back to the company and displayed to them her dorsal hump.

"In his service," she said in her rasp of a voice. "In his service I have become crooked and bent. In my father's house my back was straight. In Yankev's service it became bent. Yankev has a right to insult me, I've earned it from him."

She exhibited her twisted back, making sure everyone at her table had a good look. Like a mannequin displaying to a roomful of buyers some latter feature in haute couture, so Henye pirouetted and spun before them, pointing to the hump on her back.

The collection was titillated by this turnabout in the evening's advancement. They applauded her. She was given a handclap. "Good for you, Henye! Give it to him!"

Yankev was stunned. Dumbfounded. But only momentarily. Quickly his surprise gave way to anger.

"Cover yourself!" he bellowed. "Cover yourself, you shameless old Jezebel! In my service!" he thundered. "The gall of the woman—"

He rose to his feet and with shoulders back and handsome head lifted high, he strutted a few steps in his kitchen like a cock. He squared himself against the wall, facing the company.

"I was a stunning youth! You should have seen me at twenty-one, I was like a tree! Tall, straight, a head of hair like a lion, a neck like a bull." He pointed an accusing finger at Henye, who was hooking herself up at the back.

27

"She became bent in my service? A lie! In her father's house she was straight? A lie! As you see her now, so she was when I beheld her the first time. On my word, my friends, no different. One look at this picture my father had picked for me and I was taken with the ague. One minute I was cold, the next minute hot—"

"Enough!" came Yudah's voice from the assembly. "Enough, Yankev."

Yankev turned an astonished face to his brother. "You turn on me too? Is this Yudah, my second self, who speaks? Is this Yudah who volunteered out of pity for Yankev to stand in his place under the canopy?" Without another word Yankev took his place again at the head of his table.

Henye, her own effrontery having gone to her head like wine, was not through with him yet. (Social ascendancy over Yankev was a potent draught.) Buttoned up now but unmindful of the kettle, she spoke up again.

"No need," she said. "There was no need for Yudah to step into Yankev's place, and there was no need for Yankev himself, if I was so unpleasing to him, to take me for his wife. There were others," she said, preening almost. "One of my suitors died after I married Yankev, and left his curse on me for disappointment. I lost two children. I went to his grave after Alter was born, to beg his pardon—"

Yankev leapt to his feet, revivified. "True! She went to beg his pardon. It's my pardon she should have begged, not his. He was lying undisturbed, unplagued—and she went to beg his pardon. He was liberated, I was in bondage—it's Yankev's pardon she should have asked. Yankev!" he cried, bringing his fist to his chest and thumping himself like Tarzan.

Henye had had her brief moment. Now it was over and the company was restored to Yankev's sway.

WHEN I KNEW THE BROTHERS, their fish-peddling days were behind them. It was during Prohibition and they were making an easier dollar peddling illicit booze. The fish cart, however, was still in use. For deliveries. The topmost tray, concealing the bootleg booze in the interior of the cart, contained for the sake of camouflage a few scattered pickerel, a bit of pike, a piece of whitefish packed in ice. Yankev, to accommodate expanding trade, had a phone installed in the hall of his house and it rang at all hours, a customer at the other end asking for Jack. Their customers, for the most part Gentile, could not get their tongues around Yankev so they called him Jack. Yudah was called Joe.

The brothers had acquired a bit of English, enough to see them through their business. Their inventory and records were kept in a lined exercise book, in Yiddish. Customers were designated by descriptive terms, nicknames: The Gimpy One on Bathurst, Long Nose on Lippincott. Using their fish carts mocked up with a scattering of moribund fish in the topmost tray, they made their deliveries to Big Belly, Short Ass, The Murderer, Big Tits, The Pale One, The Goneff, The Twister, The Tank.

They operated a long time without running afoul of the law, but were apprehended eventually on a delivery run, and took a pinch, which resulted in a fine. A sobering experience this, their first skirmish with the law, and despite loss of revenue and the clamouring of customers, the brothers lay low for a while, then started up again. The fish cart, now that the cops were on to them, was held to be unserviceable, so they bought a car and Yankev learned to drive it. Yudah, of a more nervous disposition than his brother, never learned to drive.

Again they went a good time unmolested by the law, and suddenly were fallen upon, nabbed by a pair of plainclothesmen as they were loading the car. The load was confiscated and the brothers, in full view of neighbours who had come out to watch, were hustled into the squad car.

Henye was petrified. Frightened that she'd be hauled up too, she scurried for a hiding place, hollering, "*Gevald!*"

On the books a second time, the brothers drew a stiffer fine. Further, Yankev was prohibited from keeping so much as a single bottle of whisky on his premises, with a warning from the bench that a third offence would result in a jail sentence.

This gave the brothers a jolt. They were really shaken up. But it didn't stop them from selling. They kept to their course—but with more caution than before. Yudah, with a few bottles stashed on his person, would by foot or by streetcar, depending on his landing place, make a discreet delivery. Yankev, equipped likewise, would take Henye for a ride in the car. Which she loved. "In a car I could ride to Moskva," she used to say. Yankev made a few stops en route, explaining he had to collect some money owing him, and with the motor running she sat quite content waiting for him. An unwitting shill, and terrified of the law, Henye accompanied her husband on his deliveries and never tumbled that she was fronting for him.

And so things went till one Friday, with the brothers at *shul* and Henye at her pots, two plainclothesmen, without a search warrant or even a knock on the door, came directly in and began taking the place apart, looking for booze. Henye hollered, "*Gevald!* A pogrom!" and fainted. Her daughter-in-law Lily, screaming, came running down the stairs with Pesach close on her heels. The cops continued their search. Unearthing a couple of cases which they stored in their car, they sat themselves on the verandah, awaiting the brothers' return.

The shame of it! People coming from synagogue and police on the verandah as if waiting for a pair of bandits. Henye banged her head on the wall. "Let them wait inside!" she cried, and as Pesach went to fetch them she hid herself in the toilet.

The brothers came in and before the law could put an arm on either of them, Pesach, youngest of the sons and quickest in the head, made a verbal deposition to the cops. He claimed the whisky was his. Which flummoxed the cops. Briefly. All three were taken to the station, all three booked, and Monday when the case came before the bench Pesach stepped forward and taking his oath on the Bible swore the whisky was his. And with the help of a lawyer, made the story stick. Pesach drew a fine for keeping liquor on convicted premises declared by the law to be out of bounds.

The same night, and at Henye's behest, a family conclave made up of Yankev's five sons with their wives, Malke with her boyfriend the druggist, Yudah's four children with their partners, all talking at once exhorted the brothers to put an end to the business. Now that they were known to the law, it was too risky. Both were well fixed with money in the bank, they were getting a good income from the two pieces of property they had bought, Yudah had only himself to provide for, Yankev with a paid-up house was getting rent from Pesach, Malke was paying board. The brothers were reminded they were sick men, both. (They had become asthmatic in the last few years, with an advancing seriousness of chest congestion. A fright, a scare, the least bit of physical exertion brought on a fit of coughing, a whooping, strangling seizure alarming to behold.)

The brothers gave up the booze. They were together all day as before, but now there was no occupation for them, nothing to do with their time. They played checkers by the hour, casino, and went more often to the synagogue.

In the spring of that year they sat on Yankev's verandah drinking a glass of tea sweetened with slices of peeled apple. I used to bring my homework to Yankev's verandah and would hear them talking nostalgically of the bootlegging days. They missed the action. "The day is like a year," said Yankev. "But for that old devil of mine we'd still be in business."

Augusta Avenue was a busy street and the brothers, to invent a bit of diversion for themselves, sat on the verandah making asides to each other about the passersby going to and coming from the market. Their eye one day was caught by a new nose in the neighbourhood, a big woman with an excessive bosom, her breasts under a cotton dress swinging free and unleashed. The brothers gawked. Yankev nudged Yudah. "If one of those should fall on your foot, God forbid—every bone would be crushed." They fell over themselves, winded, short of breath from laughing. "*Och toch toch*," they gasped, gulping for breath, pummelling themselves on the chest. "*Och toch toch.*"

Unperceived by the brothers, Henye had come out with a pot of fresh tea. In one wink she took in the scene. "Shame on you. A pair of old men. Shame on you both," she said and spat.

Slowly Yankev turned his head in her direction. "To look, you old devil—is that forbidden too?" He snatched the teapot from her hands. "Get back in the house, I'll pour out myself."

IN THE SUMMER of that year Yudah fell sick. Painfully congested and unable to speak, he lived only nine days. People came to the house of *shivah* to comfort Yudah's children, the bereaved brother, and it was remarked by them that Yankev overnight had become an old man. When *shivah* was over, Yankev came every morning to the synagogue above which we had rooms to say *kaddish* for his brother, and fell into the habit of coming upstairs after prayers to while away some time with his niece Chayele. He used the side door of the synagogue, which gave secondary access to our place, a short climb, eighteen steps in all, but for Yankev a laborious ascent. You'd hear his *"och toch toch"* as he paused every few steps.

One morning before sitting down to his tea he extracted from the inside pockets of his coat three bottles of whisky. "A little favour, Chayele," he said to my stepmother, "to put away for a couple of days these few bottles."

"With pleasure," she responded, and hid them in the far end of the dark hall in an unused bunker filled with junk. He thanked his niece, and to me he gave ten cents not to say anything to my pa.

Next morning he came as usual for his glass of tea and before leaving took a bottle from the bunker and put it in his pocket. In a few days the bunker, denuded of booze, was replenished. With six bottles. In a short while (the bunker unable to accommodate the increasing supply) whisky was being stored in the room my sister, my brother and I slept in. A few bottles under the bed I shared with my sister, a few bottles under my brother's bed.

Two or three times a day, except on the Sabbath or a Jewish holiday—and never when my father was home—Yankev made his sorties to and from our place.

People remarked on the change in Yankev. They said he was becoming his old self again.

One day in the late fall on a Jewish holiday, with the synagogue packed out and a few members of the congregation standing out front in their prayer shawls taking a breather, a squad car drew up and two cops emerged, making straight for the outside door abutting the synagogue, which was the primary entrance to the stairs leading to our place. A quick inspection uncovered bottles in the bunker and bottles under the beds. They began querying my stepmother, who didn't understand a word they were saying.

"Ask her what's all this whisky doing here," they instructed me. "Ask her who it belongs to."

I put the question to my stepmother, then gave them her reply. "She says she can't give you a straight answer because her head is spinning with fright. She wants you to take the whisky and go before my father comes home."

They told me to ask her this, to ask her that, and as I was saying for the twentieth time, "She would like you to take the whisky and go before my father comes home," we heard his step on the stairs.

Without preamble, my father was taken over the hurdles. They told him right off they knew the whisky was not his. They knew who it belonged to, but that didn't absolve him from guilt. His place was being used as a drop. "What do you get paid for keeping?" they asked him.

"I am not in a court of law," said my father (showing off his English). "In my own house I don't have to answer any questions."

"Okay, let's go," they said, and my father, before going submissively downstairs with the cops, gave hell to my stepmother in Yiddish.

Doing my stepmother's bidding, I ran to Yankev's house with the intelligence. Yankev and Henye with their daughter, Malke, and her boyfriend, the druggist, were at supper.

Yankev clapped a hand to his forehead. "A *klog!*" he wailed. "A *klog!*"

Henye set up a holler. "He's been selling again! He wants to bury me, that *Poshe Yisroel.*"

Yankev, beating his hands together, lamented his fate. He was certain my father would open up, sell him down the river. A third conviction meant jail. Asthmatic as he was, he would never survive even a short term in jail. He would die there like a dog. His life was in the hands of the Rumanian Beast (his name for my father behind his back). "A frightening contemplation," he moaned. "Frightening."

My stepmother came running. Pa had called from the station. From what she understood he never told on anybody. He took the blame on himself—but somebody had to go right away to the station with five hundred dollars. "Bail," she said. The word had been dinned into her head.

"Thank God!" said Yankev. "The Almighty One has not forsaken me after all."

And with my father cooling his heels in the pokey, Yankev sat down to finish his supper. "Now another problem comes up," he said, drinking his second glass of tea. Who was to go to the station? He didn't dare put a nose in there. And neither did Pesach with a conviction against him. Malke's fiance rose from his place. "I'll go," he said.

"Finish first," said Yankev, pointing to the druggist's dish of compote. "The jail isn't on fire."

My father was tried, and because of the inside door of the synagogue giving secondary access to our rooms, was convicted and fined for keeping whisky in a place held by the law to be public.

Yankev put up the money for the fine, and the same evening his sons came to their father's house to upbraid and lecture him. They said they were surprised that their father, a man of principle, would go back on his word. And Yankev listened acquiescently and attended their words without demur. "A mistake," he conceded, "a mistake." Henye snorted.

Next day friends and relatives came in their numbers, and Yankev, constrained to give an ear to them too, acknowledged he was ashamed of having gone back on his word. Henye, filling the kettle, gave out a short, derisive laugh. Except for a muttered *"Gazlan!"* as she set her husband's glass of tea before him, she had nothing to say.

In the following months Yankev became soft as butter. Henye's days became easier; he had stopped belabouring her. He let up on her altogether. When company came she still kept to her corner chair, but she could open her mouth now without being jumped on.

In January Yankev fell ill and was taken by ambulance to hospital. First day he was allowed no visitors. Second day only his wife was permitted in the sickroom. Henye sat by his bed, peering at him through the oxygen tent and crying.

"Don't mourn me, I'm still alive," said Yankev and signed to her to go.

His third day in hospital his children were allowed in two at a time, and on the fourth day (Saturday) it was given out to them by the doctor that their father was very low.

Saturday noon we had a hysterical call from Pesach. His father was dying, he said, and requested of my stepmother that I be sent right away to fetch Henye. Yankev was asking for her.

When I came to Henye with my tidings, she was sitting at the kitchen table drinking tea from a saucer. I told her I had come to take her to the hospital. "Yankev wants to see you," I said. She put her saucer down and with hands clasped loosely in her lap studied my face. "Yankev sent for me?" she said in her harsh voice. I waited for her to get ready but she continued at table, rocking back and forth and muttering to herself. I caught the words *mechilah betten*, to beg forgiveness. She rose abruptly from her chair and a minute later returned in her coat and shawl.

We trudged through the snow, Henye with shawled head thrust forward holding onto my arm and keeping up a hoarse monologue on our way to the hospital.

"So the time of reckoning has come and Yankev sends for his wife. *Mechilah betten*," she said, nodding her bent head. "What is there to forgive? Everything—and nothing. Without Yankev I'll be alone. Alone like a stone. I have children—God give them health—but children are one thing and a husband is another. A husband is a friend, my dear. So Yankev hollered at me, called me names— that's nothing, it's soon forgotten. Like last year's snow. I had my faults too. Yankev was an open-handed man and I was a—" she gave me a sideways glance—"I know people called me a stingy," she said, using one of the few English words in her vocabulary. "And also other faults.

Sinful faults nobody knows about except Henye. Jealous, jealous, jealous. All my life jealous," she said with a rueful shake of her head. "People liked Yankev, I was jealous. My sister-in-law Lippa was pretty, I was jealous. People said Lippa is like a little doll, I ate my heart out. Least little thing, I laid the blame on Lippa. Yankev loved his brother Yudah, again jealous. I tried many times to come between them—"

She stopped to kick snow from her shoes, then passed under her dripping nose the handkerchief she used on the Sabbath bound around her wrist like a bandage, and we continued.

"People said Yankev doesn't like his wife—what do people know? You're a young child so you won't understand," she said (I was fourteen), "but if a woman is disliked by her husband, uninviting to him, she cannot give him even one child—let alone eight children. I was very sick when Malke was born, and who looked after me? Not my sister and not my mother. Yankev. Who fed me from a spoon like a baby? Yankev. He went two miles by foot to buy me an orange."

We came in sight of the hospital; she stopped to take a dab at her eyes with the back of her handkerchief-bandaged wrist. Being the Sabbath, Henye would not ride the elevator so we walked the four flights to Yankev's room. She searched the faces of her children who were standing in the corridor, then opened the door to her husband's room. She stood by his bed, looking at him; he appeared to be asleep.

He opened his eyes and motioned her to sit down. "Henye," he said, "I have a request—"

Henye leaned forward. "No need, Yankev. All is forgiven—"

"Good," he said, nodding his head. "Good."

"And I beg your forgiveness," she continued. "I beg your forgiveness for—"

"What is this?" he said, looking at her in puzzlement. "I'm not dying yet. You'll have plenty of time to ask for my forgiveness."

"The children said you sent for me? I thought, God forbid—"

He laughed. "*Och toch toch,*" he gasped, pummelling his chest. Henye handed him his glass of water. "Don't worry, I'll climb out. My time isn't up yet," he said, sipping water from his glass. "I sent for you to tell you something—but I don't want the children to know, you hear?" He paused to summon breath. "The last few weeks I took a little order here, a little order there—"

Henye gaped.

"In the summer kitchen behind the new bag of potatoes," he continued, "you'll find a few bottles—" he paused for breath—"so if a customer phones—"

Henye didn't wait to hear the rest. With Yankev still talking, she rose to her feet and the next minute she was out of the room.

"Come," she said, taking hold of my arm. And to her children clustered outside their father's door, "He'll live," she said.

Holding onto my arm, Henye sped along the snow-covered streets. I had to run to keep pace with her. She opened the door to her house and beckoned me to follow. Speeding through hall, through kitchen, she proceeded to the back of the house lean-to, which they called the summer kitchen. This small area used as a storehouse contained the Passover pots and pans and dishes, jars of preserves, bushel baskets of apples, onions, carrots, and in a corner of the summer kitchen two burlap bags of potatoes; the one in use easy of access, the unopened one wedged in the corner and barricaded behind several earthenware crocks containing pickled cucumbers, beet borscht and kvass.

Seizing hold of it by its neck, Henye lifted the foremost bag of potatoes, thrust it aside, then stooped to the earthenware crocks (which had to be shifted in order to gain access to the hindmost bag of potatoes). I watched Henye, a little gnome with black shawl sweeping the floor, grappling with the unwieldy crocks.

"You try," she said. "Young hands are stronger."

Tilting the crocks and rolling them on their rims, I managed, with Henye clearing space for them, to open a passage wide enough to admit a burlap bag of potatoes. Together, we pulled the bag from its lodging and there, as Yankev said she would, Henye found a few bottles. Four. She took two bottles and bade me to take the other two. "Come," she said, and I followed her to the kitchen.

She pulled the shawl from her head and took off her coat. "Open up a bottle," she directed me. She took the bottle to the sink. "Here's a customer for you, Yankev," she said, and emptied it down the drain. She told me to uncap another one. "Here's another customer," she said, and that too went down the drain. A third bottle was emptied. Draining the last one down the sink, she turned her head to me. "When it comes to whisky, Henye is not a stingy," she said slyly.

"I would give you something," she said, thanking me, "but *Shabbos* I don't carry money." Then as I made to go, she called me back. She pulled open a drawer in which she kept odds and ends, her pills, her medicines and the knotted handkerchief with its nickels and dimes. "Take ten cents," she said, pointing to the knotted handkerchief. I took hold of the knot and applying the technique I had seen her use so many times—a tug, a twist, a pull, a pluck—went to work on it. I couldn't even loosen the knot, let alone untie it. I returned the handkerchief to the drawer. "You'll pay me tomorrow."

THREE DAYS LATER Yankev came home.

Company came the same night to welcome him home. Henye bustled and scurried about. Unbidden, she brought fruit to table, cake, and made tea.

"What an escape," said Yankev, shaking his head. "To scramble out of their hands—a deliverance, my friends," he said solemnly. "A deliverance."

With Yankev home, the phone began ringing again. One night at supper the phone rang and Henye went to it. The call was for Jack. "Jeck?" she said. "Jeck not home. In Hallyefacks," she said and hung up.

For the first time since coming home, Yankev showed anger. "Don't make a fool of me, Henye!" he said as she resumed her place. "Attend to your business and leave my business to me—"

"His business," she said. "It's my business too. You took me in for a partner, you forgot? Last Saturday in the hospital when you sent for me—you don't remember? You told me where the whisky was, you told me to attend—and I did. When I came home, a customer was waiting so I gave him the whisky."

Yankev stared. "A customer was here? In the house?"

Henye pointed to the sink. "That customer."

Yankev rose and made his way to the summer kitchen. He returned and without a word took his place at table. Henye, undisturbed, continued with her food. She poured him a glass of tea and dropped into it a heaping spoonful of cherry conserve. "You saw for yourself there's no more whisky?" she said. He made no reply. She poured some tea from her glass into her saucer. "We're out of business, Mister Jeck," she said, bringing her saucer to her lips—and Yankev, despite himself, began to laugh. "*Och toch toch*," he gasped, and signalled her to get him some water. "You old devil," he said, his breath restored, "you'll be the death of me yet."

"Don't worry, Yankev," she returned, "you'll bury me."

HENYE'S WORDS WERE PROPHETIC; two months later she died in her sleep.

I went with my stepmother to Henye's funeral. With the service at the open grave concluded, Yankev took hold of the shovel. "So swift, Henye, so fast," he said, shovelling earth on the coffin. "You left in such a hurry there was no

43

time for me to ask your forgiveness. I ask it now. Intercede for me, Henye," he said, then handed the shovel to his oldest son, Alter.

People came all week to the house of *shivah* to comfort Henye's children and her bereaved husband. Henye was lauded, praised to the skies. Her children, concurring, wept at every mention of their mother's name, while Yankev, obsessed with the speed of Henye's departure, talked of it without beginning and without end.

"So fast," he said. "Like a whirlwind. We ate supper, we talked of Malke's wedding next month, how much will it cost for the hall, how much for the music—"

Malke began to cry. Her father gave her a baleful look and continued. "All of a sudden she said, 'I feel like to go to bed.' Henye to go to bed before twelve, one o'clock? Henye to leave dishes on the table? I went up myself to bed an hour later, maybe two hours later—who can remember— and she was asleep. Of that I'm sure. She turned around when I put on the light. In the morning she was cold." He struck his forehead with the palm of his hand. "When did she die? Of what? And without a word?"

Six months after Henye's death Malke was married to her druggist. With Malke gone, Yankev sat at Pesach's table Friday after shul for the Sabbath meal. Now and then Lily's mother, an active widow, a big woman who drove her own car, spoke English and lived in an apartment, made a fourth at Pesach's table for Friday-night supper—and it was observed by Pesach that his father seemed more animated the nights the widow came for supper.

Before long it was put about that Yankev was going to remarry.

One afternoon we heard the familiar "*och toch toch*" on the stairs, giving notice of Yankev's approach. Without any waste of time he told my stepmother what was on his mind. "The truth, Chayele, will I be making a fool of myself?"

"Why a fool?" my stepmother replied.

"People will laugh," he said. "Yankev a *chossin* in his old age—"

"Let them laugh," said my stepmother. "What kind of life is it to be alone?"

In March, a year to the month of Henye's death, Yankev was married and went to live with his new wife in her apartment. Three months went by and not a word from Yankev. My stepmother began to worry. She handed me a scrap of paper with Yankev's new phone number. "Phone," she said.

His wife answered the phone. "Yankev went for a stroll," she said in English. "Tell your mother I'll be going to the market tomorrow and I'll drop him off at your place."

Next morning we heard Yankev making his ascent. He came to the kitchen spruced up in a navy-blue suit. "*Och toch toch*," he gasped, fanning himself with a panama hat. "I'm not used any more to steps—in the building we have an elevator."

My stepmother fussed over him. She made tea, complimented him on his attire, his looks. "You lost a little weight, Yankev?"

"Lost a little weight," he repeated. "She put me on a

45

diet. Gives me grass to eat." (His word for lettuce.) He pointed to his glass, indicating it was to be filled again. "It's good to drink tea again from a glass," he said. "She gives me tea in a cup. What taste is there to a glass of tea in a cup? Chayele. Chayele, Chayele," he said, shaking his head and sighing.

My stepmother was disturbed. "You're not happy?"

"Happy," he echoed. "It's like you said—what kind of life is it to be alone?"

All at once he was his old self again. He smiled at my stepmother, a look of mischief coming to his face. "She bought me a pair pyjamas," he said. "Yankev sleeps now in pyjamas, and his missus like a man sleeps also in pyjamas. First thing in the morning she opens up a window and makes exercises. First of all she stretches," he said, demonstrating with his arms aloft. "Then she bends down and puts her ass in the air. And that's some ass to put in the air, believe me. And all day, busy. Busy, busy, busy. With what? To make supper takes five minutes. Soup from a can, compote from a can—it has my *boba*'s flavour. A piece of herring? This you never see on the table, she doesn't like the smell. A woman comes in to clean—with what is she busy, you'll ask? With gin rummy. True, gin rummy. They come in three or four times a week, her friends, to play gin rummy. They cackle like geese, they smoke like men. 'Dear,' my wife says to me, 'bring some ginger ale from the frig, the girls are thirsty'—she hasn't got time to leave the cards. Girls, she calls them. Widows! Not one without a husband buried in the ground," he said with sudden indignation.

"Dear, she calls me, *nu?* Before me there was another Dear and she buried him. Once in a while without thinking, I call her Henye. She gets so mad, oh ho ho. So I make a mistake sometimes, it's natural. How does a man live with a woman all his life and blot out from his memory her name—"

He rose suddenly from his chair, took a handkerchief from his pocket and blowing his nose in it went to the mirror over the sink and peered in it, dabbing at his eyes. "Cholera take it," he said, "there's something in my eye." My stepmother looked away; next minute we heard the sound of a horn. Yankev went to the window. "There she is, my prima donna." He embraced his niece. "Drives a car like a man," he muttered and took his leave.

THE NIGHT WATCHMAN

"HOW DOES IT FEEL to be a property owner?" I asked Pa Friday night at supper.

He smiled. "I came from Rumania expecting I'll make my fortune in the new world. Only I didn't expect it will take me so long." The week before, he, in partnership with his son-in-law, had bought the house in which he had been a tenant ten years.

All his years since emigrating from Rumania, Pa, untaught, unskilled in any particular craft or trade, had eked out a living of sorts at one job or another. He was a hard and willing worker, and to keep his family from want he took jobs that were not always to his liking. He was a man of short temper, and his pride—a pauper's pride—was a prickly one. Sensitive to a discourtesy, a rebuke, he would on occasion lose his temper and his job. One summer when we were small and he was out of work, he invested the last of his money in a supply of needles, thread, yarn, thimbles, measuring tape, chalk, and peddled his wares from door to door. But not in his neighbourhood; his pride hastened his steps to an outlying district, to do his drumming there. It was a poor living, peddling needles from door to door, but for want of something better, he kept to his course. One day, canvassing a well-to-do district, he rang the doorbell of a prosperous-looking house, and the lady of the house came to the door. After casting a brief glance at his wares, she went indoors, telling the peddler to wait. She returned shortly, said she was not in need of anything in that line, and offered him a dime. The peddler shut his suitcase, politely raised his hat, and leaving the lady of the house standing on her verandah with a dime in her hand, he went home and made a gift of his stock-in-trade to his wife. He was out of work again, and jobs were scarce. People went on relief; Pa hustled to find work. Picking up a short-term job here, seasonal work there, he kept himself employed and his family didn't go hungry.

"What didn't I do to make a living," he said. "Not to go on relief, I took any job I could find. And my children," he said, looking at us, "they didn't have to go hungry to bed."

True, we did not have to go to bed hungry. Practised in economy, Ma knew all there was to know about keeping a family of five fed on an unsteady housekeeping allowance. And while you didn't sit down to a deluxe spread at her table, you didn't go away from it hungry after a plate of beet borscht, a piece of herring with a boiled potato, a good helping of *mamaliga* topped with sour cream, a cup of tea. A thick barley or bean soup, a stew made of ox heart and lung, a serving of *mamaliga* to go with it, apple sauce for dessert, and you left her table replete. *Mamaliga* (corn meal cooked to a thick consistency) was an assured staple at her table. It was filling, it stayed with you. Hot, it went on the plate with a piece of boiled beef and boiled navy beans. When there wasn't any meat, it was good on its own with a bit of butter or chicken fat on it. Cold, it was good with almost anything. Pa ate it with a raw onion.

"I remember all the different jobs you had," said my sister, Bella. "You had a job in a warehouse, a job in the stockroom of a shoe store, a job in a grocery store, a job —"

I interrupted. "I remember the broken biscuits Pa used to bring home from the grocery store."

"He did not!" said Bella. "Pa used to bring us popcorn."

To Pa she said, "When we were kids, you were always changing jobs."

"I was still a young man," he replied, "so I looked for an opportunity to better myself."

Seeking to better himself, over the years Pa had left several jobs in favour of others, but the changes seldom yielded the advantage he was on the lookout for. If he happened to strike it lucky, as he did one year when he changed jobs on two separate occasions (and each time to his advantage), misfortune followed him like a shadow. The first advantageous changeover was when he left a job as marker for a cleaning and dyeing establishment for a promising job in a toy factory. He worked three months for The Original Toy Company, was promoted from worker to foreman, and the plant burnt down. And again when he left a poor-paying job for a job as conductor on a TTC streetcar, that too went by the board a few months after he was hired, when the cars with two men operating them were taken off the tracks and new ones put into service, with one man functioning as motorman and conductor. Being let out by the TTC was a blow to Pa. He looked for work, cursing his fate.

After being out of work several weeks, he was put in the way of a good job by Mr. Grober, with whom he played pinochle in the back room of Grober's Ice Cream Parlour on Augusta Avenue. Grober's brother-in-law, Moe Blum, owner of Moe Blum's Bargain House Furnishings, a small establishment that sold house furnishings on credit, was looking for a collector, and Grober recommended Pa. To qualify for the job, Pa had to learn to ride a bicycle. He bought a second-hand wheel, and early one evening when traffic had subsided he mounted the wheel and began rockily pedalling, Grober running behind with a fast grip on the saddle.

In a week's time Pa, going on forty-one, had learned how to handle a bike. "When I first got to know Bella, you were a collector," said Bella's husband, Henry. "For a Mr. Blum, wasn't that his name?"

"That's right. When you came to my house for the first time, I was already working four years for Mr. Blum. A very fine man. He talked like a roughneck," Pa said, smiling. "But he was a gentleman."

Bella was fourteen and I eleven when Pa went to work for Blum. And shortly after, reasonably sure of steady employment, Pa moved us from our lodgings which consisted of two rooms and a kitchen above a synagogue, and we took up residence in a house across the street (the house he was to buy in partnership with Billy ten years later).

The removal was effected with the help of Bella and me and a coloured man who did odd jobs in the neighbourhood. We carried the kitchen table across the street, the kitchen chairs, our clothes, bushel baskets filled with dishes, cutlery, pots and pans, bedclothes, odds and ends. Pa and the coloured man carted the heavier pieces across, the stove, kitchen cupboard and the beds. Ma too lent a hand. She took her broom across the street, kitchen mop, pail, washboard, her iron. Her clothes she carried across over one arm, with Pa's clothes over the other arm.

There were five rooms in the house, kitchen and two rooms downstairs, two rooms and bathroom upstairs. By a stroke of luck, the house had become vacant at an opportune time, and it gave Pa pleasure that it was in his power to decently settle his family. For bedrooms he apportioned to each of the girls a room upstairs. Himself and wife he put in the room at the front of the house downstairs. The kitchen and the bedroom he had allotted to himself and wife were adequately furnished with the furniture he had brought from our former lodgings. To dig up some money for furnishing the girls' rooms and the middle room downstairs, he went to the Mozirer Sick Benefit & Loan Society, of which he had in the nick of time become a member, and applied for a loan.

Meanwhile, Bella and I were clamouring for our rooms to be furnished. (The furnishings of our former bedroom, which consisted of the bed we had shared since childhood, a small table, a chair and a three-legged stool, had arbitrarily been put in the room assigned to Bella.) Neither of us

53

knew what it was to sleep in a bed by ourself in a separate room, and both were impatient for the experience of sole occupancy.

When the loan was approved, Pa, with money in his pocket, set out to buy furniture. Ma followed him to the door with blessings; Bella and I, with importunings. Among other things, each wanted a dresser (or bureau, as it was then called) for her room.

For the middle room downstairs, which was bare but for the picture (left on the wall by former tenants) of majestically robed Mary, Queen of Scots kneeling with lace-capped head to the executioner's block, he bought a round dining table, two chairs with imitation-leather seats, four mismated mahogany chairs, a white cloth for the table, lace panels for the two windows, and—as a surprise for us—a small radio. For our rooms he bought a second bed, two chairs, blinds for the windows, a bureau, and as he was not able to stretch his money to cover the cost of a second bureau, he bought a small chest of drawers.

When he got home he told us he had been able to buy only one bureau, and it was to go to Bella, as she was the oldest. I, in compensation, was given the chest of drawers and the new bed (which was bought at a second-hand store, as was everything else).

Friday night of that week Ma blessed the candles in the dining room and served the Sabbath meal with a white cloth on the table. In celebration of the occasion, Pa brought three extra glasses to the table and gave his womenfolk a measure of wine to drink. "*L'chaim*," he said, raising his

54

glass. His wife and daughters raised their glasses. "*L'chaim.*"

"Ma had tears in her eyes," I said to Bella later that evening when I was in her room. "You didn't notice, but I—"

"I certainly did," said Bella.

"Those were tears of joy," I stated.

"Go to the head of the class," Bella returned. "Do you mind getting out of my room?"

Separate rooms, and each with a bed to herself; it had actually come to pass! We revelled in it, visited each other in our rooms (when we were on good terms) and on the whole got along better. Compared with what we had left behind, the house with three bedrooms, dining room and three-piece bathroom was a mansion. And in the excitement and pride of ownership, its defects were not at first noticed.

A few months after we had taken possession, however, Bella was complaining to Pa that the house was falling apart. She pointed out the water-stained cracks in the kitchen ceiling, paint flaking off the walls, the kitchen window with its diagonal crack patched with friction tape, the worn linoleum blistered and rucked up under the sink. The summer kitchen with its rotting roof leaking rain. The faded wallpaper in the dining room coming away from the walls in several places. The linoleum on the uneven floor so worn that its pattern of latticed roses in bloom was almost altogether erased. Window sashes needed replacing; there was hardly a window in the house that you could open without propping a stick under it. The doorbell didn't work. The tap in the bathroom sink didn't work. "I have to

wash myself leaning over the bathtub," she complained—
the girl who a few months before had been washing herself
from a pail of water in the dingy bedroom she shared with
her sister. Pa said, "I'll have to get a hold of a plumber."

"And a painter and wallpaper hanger too," said Bella.

"One thing at a time," said Pa. "I'm still paying off the
money I borrowed for furniture."

When he had finished paying off what he owed, and
Bella started pestering him again, he reminded her that
he had just laid out eighty dollars for the typing and
shorthand course she was taking at a high-priced business
school. At sixteen, when Bella was working in an office
and paying board at home, Pa, who had been steadily
employed two years as collector for Blum, was still saying,
in acknowledgement of Bella's complaints, "I'll have to get
a hold of a plumber and a painter." And left for a game of
dominoes or cards, content that the hiring of the plumber
and the painter was as good as done.

"He was a gentleman," repeated the night watchman-
cum-property owner, nostalgically reminiscing about Moe
Blum, for whom he had worked six years as a collector. "He
gave me respect and I gave him respect."

Moe Blum, thirty-five years old when Pa went to work
for him, was born in Toronto of immigrant parents. He was
a handsome man, arrogant, outspoken, friendly and easy-
going with familiars, devoted to an ailing wife to whom
he had been married ten years, and father of two children
whom he adored. The horn-rimmed glasses he wore had
one clear lens that revealed an observant brown eye; the

left lens, opaque, concealed the sightless eye he had been blinded in as a boy in a school fight. The small store he rented for his business had a desk, two chairs, a telephone, a makeshift filing cabinet, and was stocked with sheets, pillow slips, bedspreads, blankets, towels, curtains, rugs. From this supply he loaded his car five mornings a week, and set out to canvass old customers and drum up new trade.

His collector, Glicksman, mounted his wheel six days a week at eight in the morning and went the rounds of the territory Blum had covered by car, collecting payments from customers who bought house furnishings from Blum on a weekly instalment plan. (Pa came in for some criticism, riding his bike on the Sabbath; the neighbours called him a *Shabbus goy* behind his back. And six years later when his younger daughter married a *shaygetz*, they said: "The apple doesn't fall far from the tree.")

Following Blum's instructions, Pa rang doorbells and stood his ground till someone came to the door. Where there was no bell, he knocked. And kept knocking. Blum had said, "Don't be shy, Glicksman, you're not asking for no handouts. They owe money, let them pay. I'm not running no charity organization."

When Pa first went to work for Blum, it worried him when a customer who was down for a two-dollar payment gave him only one dollar; when one who should have given him a dollar gave him fifty cents. These things worried him; and though Blum gave no sign of dissatisfaction and still treated him with the same familiar courtesy as he had the very first day, Pa worried that his boss was dissatisfied with his new collector. And at the end of the day's business, when they sat down at the desk to tot up the day's take in collections—and Blum made no comment—Pa feared for his job.

"What happened to Mrs. Boychuk?" Blum asked him one night. "She drop dead or something?" Mrs. Boychuk was steadily falling behind in payments.

"She told me they're having a hard time but she'll try and do better. She isn't exactly a rich woman, Mr. Blum. I saw myself how—"

"Mrs. *Boychuk* isn't a rich woman?" Blum interrupted. "What else is new? I don't go to rich people, Glicksman," he said, fixing Pa with his good eye. "They don't need me, they can buy for cash. I haven't got any rich customers, so don't lose no more sleep over Mrs. Boychuk. Get after her."

Having worked three months now for Moe Blum's Bargain House Furnishings, Pa knew his customers didn't get any bargains at Blum's. They paid through the nose, buying on time. A poor man himself, his sympathy was with the defaulter; he tried, nevertheless, to harden himself, to take a tougher line with a delinquent. But he did not have the talent for harassing or pressing an overdue account. He took what was offered and said, "Try and do better next week please."

"That's all you got from Mrs. Andrews, fifty cents?" Blum said to him a couple of days later.

"She promised she'll pay more next week."

"She should live so, the *shikkerteh*," said Blum. "And

you didn't get nothing from Mrs. Constantino?" Pa felt his heart pounding. "Her husband was laid off." "Let him hang himself," said Blum roughly.

I can't work for that man, Pa said to himself, riding home on his wheel. I can't work for a man like that. I'll give him a week's notice and look for another job. His heart turned over at the thought that he might not so easily find another job. He was born unlucky, he reflected. When Grober had put him in the way of a steady job with good pay, he thought he had landed on his feet for a change. Counting his chickens before they were hatched, he moved to a house where the rent was twice what he had paid for our rooms above the synagogue, bought furniture on borrowed money—it caused him a pang suddenly to think what pleasure it gave his wife, now that she was able to put a meal on the table without having to pinch and scrape. He put his wheel in the side alley and went in to supper with a heavy heart.

Ma was at the stove. As always when he came from work, "You're home?" she said, smiling. His glance fell on the pot of soup on the stove, with its lid inverted. This was a habit of hers; a pot was seldom put on the stove with its lid right side up. Testily he righted the lid. "Why must the lid always be *moysheh kapoyr*?" he said irritably.

The following evening after work he sat down as usual with Blum and together they totted up the collections. Then Pa got up from his chair. "Mr. Blum—" he began.

"You're sweating," Blum observed. "And you don't look so hot. What's the matter?"

To steady himself, Pa sat down. "I'm sorry, but I have to give you a week's notice."

His boss turned in his chair and looked at him. Blum never looked sideways at you or over his shoulder; when he addressed or attended you, it was always face to face. The single piercing brown eye made Pa uncomfortable. Uneasily he said, "If you can't find a collector in a week's time, I'll stay till you'll find one."

"I can find a man tomorrow. What I want to know is why you're quitting."

"I'm not the right man for the job. I can't fight with a customer, Mr. Blum. For this job you need a harder man than me."

"I had a harder man, he should only rot. The collector before you, a burglar. He clipped me six months hand running, the *goniff*. I could of had him thrown in the hoosegow for the money he took off me. But he had me figured right, the crook—he knew I wouldn't take him to court, a Jewish sonofabitch married with three kids. I fired him, told him to get the hell out. And he had the gall to call me One-Eyed Moe, the bastard. For that, I laid him out flat. Right there," Blum said, pointing to the only clear space on the floor. "All right, Glicksman, level with me. Why are you quitting? You got another job lined up?"

Pa shook his head. "I'll find one."

"Where are you gonna find work, a man your age? There's a depression going on, didn't you hear? Come on, tell me what's biting you."

"It's like this," Pa began. "I have nothing against you

personally, Mr. Blum." Choosing his words and taking care not to give offence, he conveyed as best he could how he felt about being associated with a business based mainly on exploitation of the poor.

"So you think I'm a blood-sucker. A con man, a bluffer that takes advantage of poor people that haven't got the money to buy for cash." Pa, sitting with his head lowered, made no reply. "Well, let me tell you something about my business," said Blum. "Something which you're too new in the game yet to figure out for yourself. First of all, I buy my goods from a wholesaler. He gives me thirty days to pay. If I want a discount, I have to give him cash. Second of all, the goods my customer buys on credit is the goods I already paid for. Let's say a customer buys for twenty-five, thirty bucks. At two bucks a week—if they pay the two bucks—it'll take them thirteen, fifteen weeks to pay up. I'm running a business, Glicksman, so naturally I put a pretty good markup on my goods and take a chance that they'll pay up. Does that make me a monster? There's people in this business a lot tougher than me. They'll bust the door down and go in the house to grab a lousy sheet off the bed if a customer owes. I worked for a man like that before I went in business myself. Me, if a customer pays up half, three-quarters what they owe—" he shrugged—"*ish kabibble*, so I won't make a hundred percent profit on the deal. A customer pays up in full, it's a standoff for the fall I take with a deadbeat. And don't kid yourself, Glicksman, you get plenty of deadbeats in this business. Your Mrs. Constantino—there's a prize deadbeat, the hoor. Her

61

husband was laid off," he laughed. "Which one?"

Just then the phone rang. Blum looked at his watch, rolled his visible eye upward and reached for the receiver. Pa heard a woman's voice at the other end, followed by the sound of the receiver being slammed. "That was my wife," said Blum. "She said if I'm not home in fifteen minutes, she'll kill me."

He rose, and Pa too got up to go. "So," said Blum, "what's it gonna be? Do I have to look for a new collector?"

Wavering, Pa repeated, "I can't fight with a customer."

"Who asked you to fight? You're doing pretty good without getting tough. And the customers like you. Especially the deadbeats," Blum said, laughing. He put his hand on Pa's shoulder. "Kidding on the square, I respect your type, Glicksman. You're an honest, plain-speaking man. You're no bull-shitter, and I respect you for that. And I'm not such a bad guy to work for. Stick with me and you won't be out of work so long as I'm in business. Even if times get worse, God forbid. What do you say?"

Offering his hand to the man, whom he had the day before sized up as a man without conscience or heart, Pa said with feeling, "I will try and do my best for you, Mr. Blum."

Pa worked six years for Blum (who was to go out of business at the end of that time), and as he said he would do, he tried his best for him.

Dissimilar as they were in character and temperament one from the other, a mutual attachment developed between employer and employee. On Pa's part, there was something akin to a paternal feeling in his concern for Blum's welfare. His affection for the man who was six years his junior was almost that of a father's for a son. Blum's affection was expressed in an easier, freer, jocular manner. "*Boychik*," he affectionately called his collector who was six years older. Pa, devoted, took no offence at this over-freedom of address. Any employer but Blum calling him *boychik*, and he would have walked off the job without notice. "Deadbeat," a word in Blum's vocabulary, became a word in Pa's vocabulary. And Blum, whom Pa felt he had wronged by unfairly judging him to be a man without conscience or heart, became in his eyes the victim of the deadbeat. Following up a promise of payment, Pa frequently got up from the supper table after a hard day's work to make a third and even a fourth repeat call on a customer who said she would have money for him if he came back in the evening. And when he managed by sheer perseverance to extract a two-dollar bill from an out-and-out deadbeat, he would mount his bicycle and pedal home rejoicing as if he had drawn a winning ticket on the Irish Sweepstakes. It keenly distressed him to discover an unsuspected deadbeat in a customer he had taken to be honest. Sadly shaking his head, "She didn't look to me like a deadbeat," he would say of a customer who, after paying on the dot seven weeks in a row, had begun to give him "the run around"—another of Blum's expressions. Blum would say, "Don't waste no more time on the bitch. Screw her, let her go to hell." And clean-spoken Pa would not blink an eye; coming from Blum, coarse language fell on a benign ear.

63

In the winter he froze going his rounds on the bicycle. He came home blue with cold, eyes watering. In the summer he sweated. In rainy weather he wore a cap and a three-quarter rain cape; the cap kept his head dry, and the cape his body. His legs from the knee down and his arms below the elbow got soaked. Once in a while Blum would telephone his collector early in the morning of a bitter winter's day: "It's a day for the Eskimos. You'd better stay home, *boychik*. I'm not going out myself, my wife won't let me."

Pa would reply: "And who's going to make my calls if I stay home?"

Blum would come back with: "If you wanna freeze your ass, that's okay by me."

"I remember the first time I came here for supper," Henry was saying. This was a night for nostalgic recall. Ma was in the kitchen washing up. Her grandson, Philip, a born cadger, was in the kitchen filling himself with sponge cake. Pa, his two daughters and their husbands were sitting at the table, reminiscing. "It was on a Friday night," Henry continued, "and I—"

"The first time you were here was on a Saturday night," said Bella.

When Bella started dating, she grew severely critical of her mother's housekeeping and of her father's indifference to repairs. Ashamed of the house, she met her date at the top of the street or in a restaurant. Bella's unwillingness to bring a boyfriend to the house did not go unmarked by Pa. It disquieted him that she was ashamed of the house, but for the sake of peace he let her behaviour go without comment.

When she was eighteen she was dating exclusively with Henry Sherman, a pharmacist whom she had met over the counter of a newly opened neighbourhood drugstore. One night when she told Pa she was going steady with a pharmacist, he expressed a desire to meet him. And when she made no response, he positively forbade his eighteen-year-old daughter to surprise him with a son-in-law who had not as yet set foot in his house.

When he came home from work one Saturday, a few days after this conversation had taken place, he found his womenfolk cleaning house. On my knees in the hall, I was scrubbing the linoleum and baseboard. Bella, her expression forbidding, was dusting and mopping in the dining room. He carefully stepped out of the way of her sloshing mop and went to the kitchen where Ma was sweeping up. She leaned her broom against the wall and laid two fingers on her lips. "Bella's *chossin*," she whispered, "he's coming for supper." On the stove she had a frying pan with hamburgers sizzling in chicken fat, potatoes boiling up in a pot with its lid inverted, covered pots with their contents stewing, bubbling, simmering—by the look of her stove, her every pot, vessel and stewpan was engaged. Pa righted her upside-down lids without getting cross and went upstairs to shave.

Punctually at six, 25-year-old Henry Sherman, a man of medium height with a dark complexion, black hair thinning on top, broad face with brown eyes and wide mouth, was at the door with his finger on the doorbell that didn't work. Pa, coming out of the bedroom dressed in his second suit, saw him peering through the window. He opened the door and offered his hand, introducing himself as "Bella's father, Mr. Glicksman." He then led him through the hall, calling up to his daughters, who had gone up to wash and change. We came down, Bella presented me, and Pa called Ma to come out of the kitchen. In clean apron and hair smoothed down with water, she approached with a hand extended to Henry.

Bella sat down, telling Henry to take the chair next to Pa's; that way he would be facing the one wall that (by some miracle of paper hanging) had its worn wallpaper still adhering to it.

Ma served Henry first, apologizing profusely for the second-rate meal she was offering, and pressing him at the same time to take more. Glancing obliquely at Henry from time to time, I ate with my head bent to my plate. Bella too ate in silence. Leaving it to our parents, who were engaging the guest in conversation, she hardly exchanged a word with Henry.

Interrogating Henry, an educated man, Pa respectfully inquired about the course he had taken in pharmacy. How many years did the course take to complete? Did the course involve some training in medical science as well? Was pharmacy a profession that attracted more Jews than Gentiles? Things like that. Henry was not a noticeable conversationalist. Questions put to him he answered briefly and to the point. Ma asked did he come from a large or small family. Replying to her in Yiddish, he informed her that he was an only child. She sighed. A mother with an only child, she said, was like a woman with one shirt to her back.

Henry got up shortly after supper and said he had to be back at the drugstore before eight. Pa shook hands with Henry, saying he hoped that next time he would be able to stay longer. Ma, shaking his hand, said, "Don't be a stranger." I got up. "It was nice meeting you." "Likewise," he returned, and Bella went to the door with him.

When she returned, Pa, standing, was drinking Henry's untouched glass of wine.

"What do you think of him, Pa?" she asked.

Putting down his glass, Pa ponderously remarked, "He looks to me like a very responsible man."

Asked for her opinion, Ma couldn't praise him enough. She had taken to him right away. She liked the way he conducted himself, like a *haimisher mensch*. And he fairly shone, he was so clean.

Pa drank down the rest of Henry's wine and took the glass to the kitchen. Returning, he announced, "He is a man you can go to table with." And having delivered what in his vocabulary of approbation was the ultimate in praise, he left for a game of double-deck pinochle.

"You looked as if the world was coming to an end," Henry was saying to his father-in-law, recalling the night Pa had told them that Blum was going out of business.

Pa nodded. "It happened over four years ago and I can still remember that terrible shock I got."

When Pa had been working six years for Blum, he entered the store one Friday evening after the day's work and saw Blum sitting at the desk with his face in his hands; his glasses were on the desk by his elbow. He put on his glasses as Pa shut the door, turned in his chair and said, "I've got bad news for you. I'm selling out, *boychik*. I'm going out of business."

Pa's knees buckled; he had to lean against the door for support. "Come and sit down," said Blum kindly. "Take a load off your feet."

Pa moved away from the door. Emptying his back pocket, he heaped the crumpled bills and change on the desk and then sat down.

Blum said, "I've got to get the hell out of this country, the climate's killing my wife." (His wife was asthmatic.) "So I'm taking the doctor's advice and moving my family to Arizona."

"I'm sorry to hear that," Pa replied, "but you have to do what's best for your wife." From his inside pocket he withdrew a thick stack of record cards bound with an elastic band; each card bore a customer's name and address, and Pa's pencilled-in figures of sums collected. Silently he pushed the heaped bills and change towards Blum, took the band off the cards and began: "Mrs. Carter on Roncesvalles, two dollars."

"Did you hear that joke about the cop that found a dead horse on Roncesvalles?" Blum said, smiling. "He had to make out a report but he didn't know how to spell Roncesvalles, so he dragged the horse over to Queen Street."

Smiling, Pa turned the card right-side down and went on to the next card: "Mrs. Craig on Wright Avenue, a dollar fifty. "

Blum opened the Accounts book and recorded under corresponding headings the amounts as Pa called them. He closed the ledger when they were finished, turned to Pa and said with a smile, "Did I ever tell you about my old man's bookkeeping system when he ran a grocery store? He bought from wholesalers on credit, and some of his customers bought from him on credit. To keep track of what he owed the wholesalers and what the customers owed him, my old man bought himself a nickel notepad and on one side he wrote, 'I owe Pipples,' and on the other side, 'Pipples owes me.'"

Pa smiled, but from his face it could be seen that his mind wasn't open to light conversation. He bent down to put the bicycle clips on his pants and then stood up. "When are you leaving, Mr. Blum?"

"I'll be out of this place next Saturday. That's a week from tomorrow," Blum said, handing him his Friday pay envelope. "The new man comes in a week from this Monday. But you'll meet him before then. I recommended you and he wants to have a look at you. He'll be here tomorrow when you come from work."

The following day when Pa returned from work, a short, fat man with bushy black hair and thick lips was sitting at the desk beside Blum, in Pa's chair. Blum got up. "Mr. Greenberg," he said to the man who was buying him out, "meet Mr. Glicksman, my collector for six years."

69

Remaining seated, Mr. Greenberg offered his hand, and turning at the same time to Blum, he said, with Pa's hand in his, "You didn't tell me he was an older man." He then turned to Pa. Withdrawing his hand, "How old are you?" he asked him in Yiddish, using the familiar thou.

Pa was affronted at the man's insolent familiarity of address. Anger accelerating the beating of his heart, he stooped to his bicycle clips to hide his agitation, and took them off with a trembling hand. Then he straightened. "I am not applying for a life insurance policy, that I have to tell you my age," he said, trying to keep his voice steady.

Lolling, crossing one short leg over the other, Mr. Greenberg said, "What are you so independent? Do you want to keep the job or not?"

For answer, Pa emptied his back pocket, heaped the crumpled bills and change on the desk, took the banded cards from his inside pocket and put them on the desk. "I'll go home now if you'll excuse me," he said to Blum. And added with a smile, "I think you're in this business long enough to know how to check over the cards by yourself?"

Mr. Greenberg shot up from his chair. "I asked you a question, Glicksman. Do you want the job or not? Give me a yes or a no."

Pa, at the door now, turned to look at him.

"Well?" said Mr. Greenberg. "I don't have to kiss your ass, you know. I can find a man half your age that'll be glad to get the job and be willing to work the same hours for less money."

Pa said, "Then you'd better start looking for a collector.

Next week, when Mr. Blum goes out from this place, I go out too."

Saturday of the following week Blum was on his way to Arizona; and for the first Saturday in six years his collector's wheel remained in the side alley, riderless.

Monday Pa was studying Help Wanted ads. There were not many, and the few that were listed he was not qualified for. Tuesday he bought both dailies. In the weeks that followed, he presented himself only at places that had openings with no experience required, and found in every case that his age was against him. Which caused him to recall Blum's words: "Where are you gonna find work, a man your age? There's a depression going on, didn't you hear?" The depression was still going on, and he was six years older now than he was then.

One morning when he had been out of work a month, he saw under the Help Wanted ads that Asher Iscovitz, a *landsman* of his—they had grown up together in Focsani— wanted a night watchman for his tobacco factory. In Rumania they had worked in the same vineyard and had emigrated within a year of each other. Same age, both immigrants with equal opportunities, neither one of them with more education than the other, or with more money in his pocket—and look at the difference in situation between them now, Pa reflected. It would embarrass him to ask Asher for a job. But why should you be ashamed? he argued with himself. You're not going to him for charity. You're looking for work, and he's looking for a night watchman. He went resolutely to the phone.

"Avrom Mendl!" Iscovitz exclaimed when Pa identified himself. "I don't believe it! Only last night we were talking about you. About the old times, when we came here a pair of greenhorns. I said to Fanny, 'I wonder if Avrom Mendl still makes his own wine.' Nobody makes wine like you, I still remember the taste. How are you anyway? What are you doing these days?"

Pa cleared his throat. "It so happens I'm not doing anything," he said. Then told the factory owner that he had been a collector six years for a very fine man who had to sell out his business last month. "I happened to see in the paper that you're looking for a night watchman, Asher, so I thought I'll give you a call."

"What are you talking about! I wouldn't insult you, Avrom Mendl. It's not a job for you. A night watchman is a job for a *goy*."

"It's honest work," Pa said, and argued that a man, even if he was a Jew, did not humble himself taking honest work.

Iscovitz said, "I won't argue with you. Be here at six. I won't be here when you come. Mr. Frankel, that's my foreman, he'll show you around. I'll see you tomorrow, Avrom Mendl. Give my regards to your wife."

Shortly after this conversation, Iscovitz telephoned his wife and told her about the call he'd had from Glicksman. "It's not right I shouldn't be here when he comes, it's his first day, so I'll be home a little later than I told you." And that evening at six, when Pa presented himself at the office of the tobacco factory, Iscovitz was there himself to receive him.

"Avrom Mendl!" he cried, embracing him. "How long since I didn't see you, five years?"

"It could be. Time passes like lightning . . . ."

"A very fine man," Pa was saying. "We grew up together in Focsani." Having finished talking up Mr. Blum, he was now lauding his present employer, Iscovitz, the tobacco factory owner for whom he had been working four years now as night watchman. "I came here first, and he came a year after me. He made a success, and"—he reached for his wine— "I can't complain."

It was getting late. Philip, who had had his fill of sponge cake, was getting cranky. It was time to go home. Bella got up. "We're going, Ma," she called. Ma came out of the kitchen. "So soon?"

Maybe Later It Will Come To My Mind

LADY! LADY!" An old man in a wheelchair at the far end of the corridor was beckoning me. I was standing at the elevator preoccupied with thoughts of my father, whom I was visiting at the Jewish Home for the Aged, and had not noticed the old man before. I took my finger from the Up button and went to him.

"Good morning," he said, adjusting his *yarmulke*. "You got somebody here?"

"My father," I said.

"Where is he?"

"On the fifth floor."

"That's in the hospital part, no?"

"Yes. He's recovering from an illness. And I've only got time for a short visit with him," I added warily. I had been trapped so often before. I had been prevailed on to make calls to delinquent sons, daughters, grandchildren; I had made trips to the kitchen with complaints about the menu; I had been asked to rustle up a doctor for somebody, a nurse, an orderly—and I was bound this morning not to become involved as I had only a short time to spend with my father.

75

The elevator came to the floor. "Excuse me," I said. "My father's waiting for me."

"So he'll wait a little minute," he said. "I want you should do me a little favour first."

"If I can, and providing it doesn't take too long."

Instead of saying what he wanted of me, he kept me waiting—quite deliberately, I could tell. He kept me waiting while he searched his pockets, brought out a match, struck it on his chair and held the flame to his stump of a cigar. Even after he got it going, he sat puffing away and slapping at the ashes on his vest.

A second elevator came to the floor. I was disposed to leave him and took a few steps towards it.

"Wait a minute," he said. "What are you in such a hurry? Your father wouldn't run away. All I want is you shall take me out in the garden." He cocked an eye at me. "Easy, no?"

I looked at the old man, taking him into account for the first time. During visits to my father I had encountered dozens of old men in wheelchairs, also old ladies in wheelchairs. I had spent the time of day with them in hallways, in sitting rooms, and had done errands for many of them. I had been thanked, excessively so, for a trifling service like addressing an envelope. For making a telephone call I had been blessed. But this man—there was something odd about him. I had never been addressed with such peremptoriness, such lack of regard for my own affairs. There was something about him that took me back. Where had I seen him? I looked at the old man, studying him. Broad face, heavy-lidded eyes, hooked nose, thick torso and short legs, his feet barely reaching the footrest of his chair.

"What are you looking?" he said, bringing me up short. "You never saw an old man before? Go behind better and give me a little push," he said in Yiddish. "The Messiah will come first before I'll come out in the garden."

Ah, now I had it! Now I knew who he was!

"Is your name Layevsky? Myer Layevsky?"

He closed an eye at me. "How did you know?"

"I used to work for you. A long time ago, about thirty years ago. I was your office lady. My name was Miss Glicksman. I worked for you nine months, and you fired me. Do you remember me?"

He wagged his big head. "From this I shall remember you? God willing I shall have so many years left how many girls I fired. So I fired you. On this account you wouldn't take me out in the garden?"

"Oh, don't be—" I was about to say don't be silly. Fancy saying don't be silly to Myer Layevsky.

I wheeled him to the lobby, and once outside the glass portals, carefully down the ramp.

"How's your son?" I asked.

He turned full face to me. "My Israel? A very important man," he said, giving equal emphasis to each word. "A very big doctor in the States."

"And Mrs. Layevsky, how's she?"

He turned, facing front. "Dead. A healthy woman crippled by arthritis. Ten years younger than me. I always had in my mind the *Molochamovis* will come for me first, but it turned out different. Take me over there by the big tree."

I settled him by the big tree. "And you don't remember me? I was only sixteen, and now I'm a married woman with two grown children, so I must have changed a lot. But you should remember me. You gave me a week's holiday. I took an extra few days, and when I came back, you had another girl in my place. Now do you remember?"

"Ask me riddles," he said, again in Yiddish. "Do me a favour and go to your father," he said, using the familiar thou instead of the formal you with which he had first addressed me. "Maybe later it will come back to my mind."

My father was in the armchair beside his bed, reading a newspaper. "Pa! You'll never guess who I saw downstairs. Remember Myer Layevsky, the man I used to work for?"

My father removed his eyeglasses. "I remember him very well. And also how you hid under the bed from him when he came to find out why you didn't come in to work one morning. Correct?"

My father had it wrong. He was confusing Myer Layevsky with Mr. Teitlbaum, the comforter manufacturer, from whom I had hidden under the bed.

"You've got it wrong, Pa," I said. "You're thinking of Teitlbaum, the comforter manufacturer. But how did you know I hid under the bed? Ma swore she wouldn't tell you."

"Maybe a little bird told me," he said. "Now I remember. It seems to me you got another job that summer. Correct?"

"That's right. For a toy factory, remember? Three days

after I quit Imperial Comforters I went to work for a toy factory, in the Kewpie Doll section. I wanted to stay on, but you wouldn't let me. You made me go back to commercial school. But I went only six weeks of my second term, and you let me quit. Then I went to work for Layevsky, the man I saw downstairs—"

"I let you quit Commercial? This I don't remember, but if you say so, maybe you remember better." He sighed reminiscently. "You always had your own way with me. Whatever you wanted you accomplished."

Like fun I'd always had my own way with him. For one thing, I never wanted to go to Commercial. My plan, after being passed out of grade eight, King Edward School, was to go with my best girlfriend, Lottie Kogan, to Harbord Collegiate, but my father wouldn't cough up the money for books. So I had to go instead to commercial school, where the books were free and the course took only two years. I loathed the sight of that dismal building, the dreary classroom, the drabs I was thrown in with, and went every morning five days a week with a resentful, heavy heart, and my lunch in a paper bag.

Sure, he let me quit Commercial after only six weeks of my second term, but not through any understanding on his part, or sympathy: I swung him around through a trick, a bit of chicanery.

EVERYTHING HAD GONE WRONG for me that Monday of my seventh week. I had gone to bed the night before with a bag of hot salt pressed against my cheek to ease a toothache, and Monday morning after a troubled night's sleep my cheek was inflamed. When the noon bell rang, I was as miserable as I had ever been in my life. When I tried to get at my lunch, my desk drawer was jammed. Propping my feet against the legs of the desk, I gave the drawer a terrific yank. It shot out suddenly, knocking me back and landing overturned in my lap. Everything spilled to the floor, pencils, pads, erasers, books. I scrabbled around collecting my things, and returning them to the drawer, noticed a man's handkerchief, dirty, clotted and stuck in the right-hand corner. I had never got the drawer more than partially open before, so it must have been there all these weeks side by side with my lunch. My tooth began to ache again. I fled the room and that night at supper screwed up enough courage to tell my father I would not be returning to Commercial.

He reared. "Why?" he wanted to know.

"Because I found something in my desk."

"What did you find?"

I made no answer; I knew under cross-examination my case would be lost. He insisted on knowing; he kept badgering me. "A dead mouse?"

"Worse."

"What worse?" he persisted, getting angry.

"Don't ask me, Pa." And on the inspiration of the moment, I turned my inflamed cheek to him and said, "I'm ashamed to talk about it."

And my father, sensing that the object had something to do with sex, stopped questioning me. I had won. I knew he'd never let me quit on account of a dirty hankie in my desk.

A week later, through an ad in the paper reading Girl Wanted, Easy Work, Easy Hours, Good Pay, I went to work for Myer Layevsky. Myer Layevsky was sitting in a swivel chair at a cluttered rolltop desk in his two-by-four office when I came to be interviewed for the job. His hat was on the back of his head, and in his mouth a dead cigar. He swivelled around, and closing one eye, inspected me with the open one.

"You're a Jewish girl, no?"

"Yes."

"I had already a few people looking for the job, but I didn't made up my mind yet." He pointed to a beat-up typewriter. "You know how to typewrite?"

"Yes."

"So if I'll give you a letter, you'll be able to take down?" He rooted around the desk and came up with several lots of file cards, each bound with a rubber band. "Customers," he said. "I sell goods on time. You heard about that joke a dollar down and a dollar when you ketch me? This is my business."

He extracted one lot of cards and put them aside. "Deadbeats," he said, screwing both eyes shut and shaking his head. "Deadbeats. From this bunch nobody comes in to pay. I have to collect myself. Sometimes I even have to go and pull back the goods, so this bunch you can forget about." He went on to the other cards. "This bunch is something different," he said fondly. "Good customers, honest people which they come in regular with a payment. So this is what you shall do. A customer comes in the office with a payment? First you'll take the money. Next you'll find out the name. Then you'll make a receipt, mark down on the card the payment, and keep up to date the balance." He struck a match on the desk and put it to his cigar. "Easy, no?

"Another thing which I didn't mention it yet," he said. "Sometimes it happens a cash customer falls in the office for a pair sheets, a pair towels, a little rug, a lace panel, something—so come in the back, I'll show you my stockroom."

I was taken by surprise when he stood up, to see how short he was. Sitting, he looked like a giant of a man. But the bulk of him was all in his torso; his legs were short and bowed, and he stood barely over five feet, and loping in baggy pants to the stockroom, he looked like a comic mimicking someone's walk.

Except for a conglomeration of stuff piled in a corner of the stockroom, everything was in order, price-tagged and easy to get at.

"This mishmush," he said, indicating the heaped-up pile, "is pulled goods from deadbeats which they didn't pay. So if a poor woman comes in the office with cash money for a pair secondhand sheets, a pair secondhand towels, a lace panel, something, let her pick out and give her for lest than regular price. Give her for half. A really poor woman, give her for a little lest than half."

Right away I panicked. "How will I know a real poor woman from only a poor one?"

"You got a pair eyes, no?" He snapped off the overhead light. "So that's all. You'll come in tomorrow half past eight."

"An office job," said Ma when I gave her my news. "Wait till Pa hears."

When Pa heard, the first thing he said was, "How much a week?"

"I forgot to ask, Pa."

"Very smart. The first thing you do," he lectured me, "is to ask how much. If he mentions a figure not satisfactory, you ask for more. The way you handled, you'll have to take whatever he gives. But it's not too late yet. You didn't sign no contract, so tomorrow before you'll even sit down or take off your coat, you'll ask him."

You'd think, to hear my father, that he was the cagey one, the astute bargainer. All his years a loyal slavey, he had worked his heart out for peanuts, protecting the boss's interest, saving him a dollar. Only the year before, my father had been out of work, and things were so desperate in the house with no money for food or rent that he went finally (and at the cost of his pride) to Iscovitz, one of his rich Rumanian connections who owned a tobacco factory. Iscovitz had nothing to offer my father except a job as night watchman.

When a heist took place, my father stood up to the thugs, and was cracked over the head for it. He lay in bed three weeks with a bandaged head and fractured shoulder.

A few days after the foiled stickup a basket of fruit came to the house with a card from Iscovitz, and one night the millionaire himself came to visit. "Take your time, Avrom Mendl, and don't worry. I don't want to see you in my place till you're better," he admonished my father, then came to the kitchen seeking my mother.

"He's a wonderful man," he said in Yiddish, and slipped her an envelope with a month's pay in it.

When I came to work, Myer Layevsky was out front loading his car. He blinked an eye at me, and I passed through to the office. Doing my father's bidding, I stood without removing my coat or sitting down. It took him a while to complete loading, and lugging goods through the office to the car he passed me several times, never once looking at me. This made me very nervous. Finally the car was loaded, and Layevsky came back. He straightened his hat and put a match to his cigar. "So I'll go now. You didn't brought a lunch?"

"I thought I'd go home," I said. "I live only ten minutes from here."

"Next time bring something to eat. I don't like the office shall be left alone. A customer comes in to pay and they find a closed office, they have an excuse to put off. Even a good customer will take advantage. Take off your coat and come in the back. I'll show you a hanger."

He was back at the door, and I hadn't got up nerve to ask about my pay. "Mr. Layevsky? I forgot to ask you yesterday. We haven't settled yet—"

"I had in my mind to pay ten," he said, "but I need a Jewish girl in my business, so you I'll give twelve."

It was late in October when I came to work for

Layevsky, and during the winter months I had to keep my coat on, it was so cold in the office. There was a hot-air register behind the door at the entrance to the stockroom, with hardly any heat coming through, and I used to stand on it stamping my feet, which were icy by midday.

"I'll tell a few words to the janitor," Layevsky kept promising, and one morning before the day's peddling, he did go down to the basement. There was a great rumbling below, and in a few minutes a rush of smoke came shooting through the register. Layevsky came back and stood over the register, rubbing his hands.

"You wouldn't be so cold no more," he said. "Comes up a little bit heat now, no?"

"You mean smoke," I said.

He blinked an eye at me. "So she has a little sense," he said in Yiddish.

THERE WASN'T ENOUGH WORK to keep me busy, and in the beginning I sat banging away at the old typewriter, getting up speed against the day he'd give me dictation. But I soon got bored with that, and one morning came to work with a book.

Layevsky spotted it immediately. "No, no, no," he said, wagging his head. "Don't bring no more a book to the office. It's not nice a customer comes in and the girl sits with a book."

"But there isn't enough work here to keep me busy," I protested.

"Who said? In an office you can always find something

to do. Check over the cards, it wouldn't hurt."

I took my coat to the stockroom, smouldering.

"Come here, my book lady," he called.

Hunched over the desk with knees bent and arms locked behind his back, he was peering at some cards he had fanned out, his nose almost touching, ashes dropping all over the place.

"Pick out Mrs. Oxenberg's card," he said.

I pointed to it.

"Pick it up, it wouldn't bite you. Now take a look."

I knew the cards were in order, but to satisfy him I glimpsed it briefly and returned it to the desk. "There's nothing wrong with this card."

"Look again," he said, thrusting it under my nose.

I resisted an impulse to slap it out of his hand, and turned my head away instead.

"Mrs. Oxenberg," he mused, "a good customer. I only wish I had more customers like that." Suddenly he slapped the card down, and with his nicotined finger, pointed to the last entry on it. "When did she made the last payment?"

"October twelfth," I said, "but that's before I was here."

"And today is already middle November, no? You can't see from the card that up till now she came in regular every week with a payment, and now it's a whole month she didn't come in? This you didn't notice? Maybe she's sick. Maybe she died, God forbid. Pick up the phone, find out. Attend better to my business, and you wouldn't find time to read a book in the office."

The first three weeks I worked for Layevsky he used

to come back from the day's peddling before five. I would vacate the swivel chair, and he would sit down to check the day's take. No matter how much the amount varied, "That's all you took in today?" he'd ask. I took it as a joke at first, a pleasantry between us, but when I got to dislike the man, I resented it. "As if I were a salesgirl," I muttered once. "Or even a thief."

"What did you said?"

"Nothing." I had a feeling as I went to the door that he was laughing at me, but I did not look back to see.

After I'd been there a month he started coming back later each day; it was seldom before six now when he returned, and I'd stand peering through the office window looking for the car.

One night he didn't get back till seven, nor had he telephoned. Cold and hungry, I was standing on the register, and through the half-open stockroom door, saw him as he came in. He took a one-eyed look around. Lights on, no one in the office. He came loping to the stockroom.

"You're still here?"

I was incensed, indignant to the point of tears. "You speak as if I'm a guest who's overstayed her welcome." I swept by him; he followed me to the office.

"I speak like a what?"

I took my handbag from the desk. He followed me to the door.

"No, earnest," he said in Yiddish. "I speak like a what? Tell me." His manner was concerned, solicitous even, but I felt he was mocking me.

"Never mind," I said. This time I did look back, and saw him laughing at me.

One day a month was given over to repossessing merchandise. He would return at day's end, and through the office window I'd see him yanking piece by piece from the car, loading his shoulders. Draped like an eastern merchant escaped from a bazaar holocaust, he loped from office to stockroom, muttering, "You can't afford? Don't buy. I don't go in with a gun to nobody. Chutzpah. When it comes to take advantage, everybody knows where to find Myer Layevsky."

One day he was muttering, mulling this over, the injustice of it, the grievance to himself, when the telephone rang. I took the phone. It was Mrs. Greenberg, a good customer, an honest woman. Where's that tablecloth? she wanted to know, the one she ordered three days ago.

"It's Mrs. Greenberg," I said, my hand over the mouthpiece. "About that tablecloth, style 902 with the lace border? I told you about it—"

He took the receiver from me. "Hello. Who? Oh, Mrs. Greenberg, what can I do for the lady? What tablecloth, when tablecloth? Who did you gave the message? Oh, my office lady," he said, swivelling around so that his back was to me. "You'll have to excuse. She's a young girl, she thinks about boys. Next time if you need something in a hurry, better speak to me."

I wanted to knock his hat off, grab the cigar from his mouth and jump on it.

Despite having been forbidden to bring books to the

office, I kept sneaking them in under my coat, and one morning, caught up in *Of Human Bondage*, I didn't hear the door. I jumped as if I'd been surprised in a criminal act; I put the book out of sight as if it were a bottle. Standing before me was a blond young man, tall, thin, with a pointed nose and white eyelashes. An albino.

"Is my dad here?" he asked. "I'm Israel Layevsky, Mr. Layevsky's son."

I told him his father would not be back before five, and loping like his old man, he went to the door. "Tell my dad I was here. And also that I came first in my class."

"Your son was here," I reported to Layevsky. "He asked me to tell you he came first in his class."

A smile came over Layevsky's face, breaking it wide open. All of a sudden he jumped up, clicked his heels together, and in baggy pants began a little dance in the office, clapping his hands. He left off as suddenly as he began, and sank to the swivel chair puffing, fanning himself with his hat. "Twenty years old and going through for a doctor already since seventeen. So better don't make eyes on him," he said, wagging a roguish finger at me, "because it wouldn't help you nothing. I'm looking for a rich daughter-in-law."

ONE FRIDAY the second week in July Myer Layevsky said, "How long do you work here now, nine months, no?"

"About that," I said.

He blinked an eye at me. "You feel you're entitled to a holiday?" He handed me a roll of single dollar bills.

89

"Count over, you'll find two weeks' pay. You don't work so hard in my place you need a holiday, but I close up anyway the office a week in July to take my missus to the country."

A holiday! The idea was thrilling. Except for day excursions to Hanlan's Point or Centre Island with Lottie Kogan, I had never been anywhere.

"So where will you go?" my father asked when I told him about the holiday.

"I don't know, Pa. I'll look in the paper under Summer Resorts."

"Don't look in the paper because I wouldn't let you go just anyplace, a young girl, and fall in the wrong hands."

I began boo-hooing, the disappointment was so keen, and ran to the room I shared with my sister, Bella, slamming the door shut. I heard him in the kitchen talking it over with Ma, but as to what was being said, nothing. I heard him go to the telephone in the hall, but he spoke into the mouthpiece, keeping his voice down. He then came to the door. "Come out, my prima donna, and we'll talk about the holiday."

"Don't bother," I said, "I'm not interested anymore."

"So what did I spend money on a long-distance call to Mrs. Rycus?"

Mrs. Rycus, another one of my father's Rumanian connections, was a widow who had a small hotel in Huntsville and took lodgers during the summer months, mostly Rumanians.

"Poor woman," Pa said anytime he spoke of her. "Lived

like a duchess in Focsani. Now it's all she can do to keep a head over water."

My sister, Bella, came home from work. She went to the kitchen, then came to the room we shared. "Pa says you're going to Huntsville? Mrs. Rycus says she can take you, but you'll have to share a room with the cook and maybe help out in the kitchen."

"That's great," I said.

"Why, what's wrong with that?" my sister said. "At least you'll be out in the country, and that's something, isn't it?"

"Have you got a bathing suit?" my father asked me at supper. "Mrs. Rycus said you'll need one."

"You mean an apron," I said, and my father flared up.

"Don't be so smart. I can still phone Mrs. Rycus and cancel."

My mother winked at me to keep quiet and not ruin my chance of a holiday.

First thing Saturday morning I went to Eaton's, and in the bargain basement equipped myself with a few assorted summer items, including a bathing suit, and Monday morning my father put me on the train for Huntsville. He fussed about securing me a window seat, then fussed again about whether it would be best to put my case on the rack or at my feet. The conductor called All Aboard, and my father unexpectedly leaned down to kiss me. His kiss, embarrassing both of us, landed on my ear. Through the window I saw him on the platform.

"Don't forget what I told you," he was saying. I was to be met by Mrs. Rycus's truck driver, Bill Thompson.

"You'll wait till a man approaches you. Don't you mention the name first," my father had warned me. "If he says Bill Thompson, you'll get in the truck with him. Have a good time," my father called, and as we pulled out, he raised his hat to me!

The station emptied quickly at Huntsville. I waited ten minutes, and the only living soul to show up was a good-looking boy, about twenty, who positioned himself inside the door, giving me the once-over. Could this be Bill Thompson? I was expecting an old man. Forgetting my father's warning, I jumped from the bench. "Is your name Bill Thompson?"

"That's right," he said, and I got in the truck with him. We drove four miles to the hotel, the truck driver all the while stealing flirtatious glances at me as I sat puffing away on the cigarette he had given me.

My father, fearful I might fall into wrong hands under Summer Resorts, should have seen this!

MRS. RYCUS, a lot shorter and greyer than I remembered, was on the hotel verandah to greet me. "Sura Rivka." She smiled, giving me my Jewish name; and stubbing out her cigarette, came slowly forward on swollen legs to embrace me. "Come, we'll go in the garden for tea," she said in an accent as thick as my father's. "Bill, take her suitcase up to Mrs. Schwartz's room." And the truck driver, picking it up, gave me a wink.

Sitting at cafe tables in the garden were about a dozen ladies, all in brightly coloured dresses, some with straw hats

92

on their heads, others with kerchiefs.

Mrs. Rycus clapped for attention. "I have a surprise for you," she said, putting her arm around my waist. "This lovely girl is Avrom Mendl's daughter."

A fluster and flurry ensued at all tables. There were cries of No! I don't believe it! So big!

Mrs. Rycus whispered, "Don't be shy, darling. These are all Daddy's friends."

Piloted by Mrs. Rycus, I was taken from table to table, each lady in turn kissing and complimenting me. I had never been called darling or kissed so much in my life. One lady, a Mrs. Ionescu, wouldn't let go of me. "Sit by me, darling," she coaxed as the tea trolley was wheeled in by a maid. The trolley contained such a variety of things, I couldn't take them all in at a glance. Sandwiches, small sausages, black olives, fruit, iced cakes, cream buns. I pointed to a cream bun, and the maid put it on my plate.

"Tea or coffee?" she asked.

"Tea, please."

"Milk or lemon?"

"Milk, please."

Wasn't this thrilling! I was with real quality now, classier by far than anything I had read about in books. I wondered if I should have said please to the maid. I had said it twice—maybe even once was infra dig?

"What grade are you in school?" I was asked by a Mrs. Kayserling.

"I'm not in school anymore. I'm working."

"Clever girl," she said. "What kind of work?"

I had got over my initial shyness and felt at ease now, on top of everything. Incorrigible showoff, I rattled away like one o'clock. "Oh, at a sort of bookkeeping job. I work for a Myer Layevsky, a very funny man. He sells goods on time."

"Goods?" another lady asked.

"Yes. Sheets, towels, blankets, Axminster rugs and lace panels. He calls it goods."

"On time?" another lady asked.

"Yes. To poor people," I said, offhandedly dismissing the poor as if my only connection with them were through my job. "It's a dollar down and a dollar when you ketch me." I loped across the lawn imitating Myer Layevsky. I blinked an eye at the assembled company. "That's all the money you took in today?" And they fell about.

After tea the ladies retired for a siesta, and I went up to the cook's room to unpack. Dinner was not till eight, and it was now only six—was I expected to help? I went downstairs and located the kitchen. Mrs. Rycus was at the stove beside a fat lady in an apron, a waitress was putting hors d'oeuvres on a tray, and Bill, in a far corner of the kitchen, was emptying a garbage container.

"Mrs. Schwartz, this is Sura Rivka, the daughter of a very dear friend, and for the next week your room companion," said Mrs. Rycus, introducing me to the fat lady in an apron. She then introduced me to Leona, the waitress.

"What can I do?" I asked Mrs. Rycus. "My father said I was to give you a hand in the kitchen—"

"Certainly not," she said. "That was Daddy's suggestion, not mine." Nothing was expected of me except I come to the kitchen in the morning and get my own breakfast. "The dining room does not open till one," she said. "The ladies don't come down to breakfast. They take a cup of hot chocolate and a biscuit or something like that in their rooms. I'm short a waitress, so if you don't mind to give Leona a hand with the trays, I would appreciate it. But only if you like, darling. Otherwise, Leona can manage herself. Meantime, go for a little walk to the beach, it's very pretty there. Bill, take the garbage to the incinerator, then show her where the beach is."

It was a fifteen-minute walk to the beach, Bill flirting with me all the way, and by the time we got there I was head over heels in love with the good-looking truck driver.

At dinner that night I was seated with Mrs. Kayserling and her husband, Aaron, who had come for a few days in the country. I came to the dining room hungry as a bear, but when I saw the array of silver at my plate I was dismayed, appalled, my appetite left me. "When I was your age I could eat an ox," Mrs. Kayserling chided me. I made out that I had a very small appetite, so small it caused my father worry sometimes.

After dinner we went to the lounge for coffee, and I sat listening to nostalgic talk of Rumania. Wonderful stories, and told for my benefit, I expect, as my father was featured in most of them. Tales of escapades, derring-do. My father? Fabulous stories, fascinating to listen to—but in the end had the effect of sending me to bed unhappy, depressed.

In Focsani my father had been on easy terms with these people, on equal footing with them. What a contrast now between their way of living and ours. He, so far as I knew, was the only failure of the Focsani emigres, the only pauper.

But I was up early next morning, happy again, restored. What was the matter with me? I was holidaying in the country and in love.

After breakfast I helped Leona with the trays, then went to the beach in my new bathing suit. I had not been there ten minutes when Bill Thompson arrived. "Mrs. Rycus sent me. I'm supposed to keep an eye on you," he said, ogling me. On the way back I let him kiss me, and remembering my first kiss, could not for the rest of the day fix my attention on anything.

Wednesday morning at trays Leona was not at all friendly. Was she in love with Bill too? Later in the day I went to market with Bill and the cook, and sat between them in the cab, thrilled at the truck-driver's proximity. Thursday morning Bill told me he and Leona were going to town that night for a movie. "See if Mrs. Rycus will let you come too," he said.

"Go, darling," Mrs. Rycus said, "there is nothing here for you to do."

Bill sat between us, and in the dark of the cinema, held my hand all through *Catherine the Great* with Elizabeth Bergner.

What a wonderful week. The excitement of being in love, the secrecy, the preoccupation, the thralldom of it. The ruses I contrived to meet my love at the incinerator for a few minutes before dinner, and again after dinner for walks along the country road . . .

But the inevitable Sunday arrived. The holiday was over. I was to leave by the six-o'clock train. I took my things from the cook's closet, snuffling over my open case. To go back to my dreary home, my miserable job, and never again to see Bill. He had said something about getting work in Toronto, but I knew for sure I'd lose him to Leona, who was prettier than me and older.

Mrs. Rycus came to the room. "I shall miss you, darling. It's such a pity you have to go back to the hot city. Wait," she said, "I have an idea. Leave everything. Go down and phone your Mr. Layevsky. Ask him to let you stay another week. It won't cost him anything. You'll stay as my guest."

I was so nervous when Layevsky's voice came over the long-distance wire, I had to make my request a second time before he understood me.

"It won't cost you anything, Mr. Layevsky. I don't expect to get paid."

"So what can I complain? Stay long as you like," he said and hung up.

That worried me, I didn't like the sound of it—but surely that was only Layevsky's way? He would have ordered me back if he didn't want me to stay.

I managed to get word to Bill. I told him at the incinerator I was staying another week, and again that night after dinner I excused myself from the lounge on the pretence of going up to bed, then sneaked down the back staircase to meet him.

**

MONDAY MORNING Leona handed me Mrs. Rycus's tray. "She wants you to bring it," she said.

I knocked, Mrs. Rycus called "Come," and I brought the tray to her.

"Sit down a minute, Sura Rivka," Mrs. Rycus said, and I took the chair beside her bed. She put her cigarette in a holder, smiled at me and began. "You're a big girl, a young lady now, and I would not presume to lecture you, but as I am such a close friend to Daddy, you won't take offence? Bill is a nice boy, but just a boy from the village. Common. He is not for you, darling, and I don't like for you to be so much with him. You understand what I mean?"

I wanted the floor to open up. I wanted to drop out of sight never again to be seen by Mrs. Rycus. I reached forward, almost toppling the hot chocolate in her lap.

"Yes, of course I understand. You don't want me to go to the market with him anymore—"

"To the market is all right, and to the pictures if Leona goes too is all right. But at night alone with him for a walk? No, darling, this worries me."

So she had known all along. I could die for shame. Talking so cleverly in front of the ladies, then sneaking down the back staircase for hugs and kisses with the truck driver.

I went to the cook's room and stayed there, ignoring the one-o'clock signal for lunch. Mrs. Rycus came up to fetch me.

"I want to go home," I bawled.

"Darling," she said, embracing me. "I could bite my tongue. You must excuse an old lady. Come down to lunch. Please, for my sake."

Next morning at her usual time she came to the kitchen with instructions for the cook. "Sura Rivka," she said, handing me a list. "If you don't mind to do me a favour, go with Bill to town. I need a few things from the drugstore, and he will not be able to attend to everything."

Bill, instead of continuing on the main road, turned sharply off onto a side road. "How come you stood me up last night? Are you playing hard to get?" He made a grab for me and tried some fancy stuff. I slapped his hand. He lit a cigarette and backed the truck onto the main road again. "You Jewish girls are all alike," he said. "There's only one thing you're after, that wedding band."

Through the corner of my eye I studied his face as he drove sullenly to town. His head had assumed peculiar contours; it looked flat on top, something I had not noticed before. I was out of love. Leona was welcome to him. I had a longing suddenly to go home. To see my father, who had raised his hat to me in the station, to see my mother, and even my sister, Bella.

After lunch I sought out Mrs. Rycus. "Please, I want to go home on the six-o'clock train. Not because of anything you said yesterday, honestly. It's just that I'm homesick."

"Darling," she said, "I understand what it is to be homesick."

Oh, I was glad to be on my way. I wouldn't have to think up funny stories to amuse the ladies at tea time. At home I didn't have to sing for my supper; I could be as glum as I pleased. My father might call me prima donna, my mother might ask if I'd got up on the wrong side of the bed.

Pa was at the station to meet me. "You had enough of the country?" he said, and we boarded a streetcar.

Next morning, apprehensive of my encounter with Layevsky, I put off going to work till nine o'clock. By nine he'd be on his way for the day's drumming, and I could let myself in with the office key.

I arrived ten past nine and through the office window saw a girl sitting at the desk. She swivelled around as I entered. She was blond, with buckteeth and eyeglasses. Definitely not a Jewish girl. I stammered, "Are you—is this—"

"This is Supreme Housefurnishings," she said briskly.

"Did you want to see some merchandise?"

"No, no," I said, collecting my wits. "I used to work here, but I've got another job now." I put the key on the desk. "I always meant to return this, but with one thing and another—"

"Thank you," she said and turned to the cards, dismissing me.

Deposed! Supplanted! It hit me like a stone.

MY FATHER HAD dozed off again. I roused him. "Pa!"

He excused himself again. "I had some pills this morning, it makes me very sleepy. We were talking about something—that man you saw downstairs."

"That's right. Myer Layevsky. He's the one that gave me

a week's holiday, and I went to Mrs. Rycus in Huntsville, remember?"

"Oh, yes," said my father. "She was a wonderful woman, Mrs. Rycus. You know we grew up together in Focsani? In Rumania she lived like a duchess, but here she had a hard time to keep a head over water."

"I'll go now, Pa, and see you tomorrow."

My father held his hand out, and as was our custom except for the time he kissed me on the train, we shook hands on leave-taking.

Myer Layevsky was still under the big tree where I had settled him. He beckoned me, and I cut across the lawn.

"Didn't I told you maybe later it will come back to my mind?"

"Then you do remember," I said, exhilarated beyond all reason.

"I gave you a week off, but that wasn't enough for you. You made me a long-distance call, no?"

"That's right. You know why I didn't want to come back? I fell in love that summer. With a *shaygetz*," I added mischievously.

That stopped him. He cocked an eye at me. "Did you married him?"

"No, I married a nice Jewish boy."

"Better," he said, nodding his head and chewing his dead cigar. "Better."

I had, in fact, married a nice Gentile boy—but there was no need for Myer Layevsky to know that.

A Basket of Apples

THIS MORNING Pa had his operation. He said I was not to come for at least two or three days, but I slipped in anyway and took a look at him. He was asleep, and I was there only a minute before I was hustled out by a nurse.

"He looks terrible, nurse. Is he all right?"

She said he was fine. The operation was successful, there were no secondaries, instead of a bowel he would have a colostomy, and with care should last another—

Colostomy. The word had set up such a drumming in my ears that I can't be sure now whether she said another few years or another five years. Let's say she said five years. If I go home and report this to Ma she'll fall down in a dead faint. She doesn't even know he's had an operation. She thinks he's in the hospital for a rest, a checkup. Nor did we know—my brother, my sister and I—that he'd been having a series of X-rays.

"It looks like an obstruction in the lower bowel," he told us privately, "and I'll have to go in the hospital for a few days to find out what it's all about. Don't say anything to Ma."

"I have to go in the hospital," he announced to Ma the morning he was going in.

She screamed.

"Just for a little rest, a checkup," he went on, patient with her for once.

He's always hollering at her. He scolds her for a meal that isn't to his taste, finds fault with her housekeeping, gives her hell because her hair isn't combed in the morning and sends her back to the bedroom to tidy herself.

But Ma loves the old man. "Sooner a harsh word from Pa than a kind one from anyone else," she says.

"You're not to come and see me, you hear?" he cautioned her the morning he left for the hospital. "I'll phone you when I'm coming out."

I don't want to make out that my pa's a beast. He's not. True, he never speaks an endearing word to her, never praises her. He loses patience with her, flies off the handle and shouts. But Ma's content. Poor man works like a horse, she says, and what pleasures does he have. "So he hollers at me once in a while, I don't mind. God give him the strength to keep hollering at me, I won't repine."

Night after night he joins his buddies in the back room of an ice-cream parlour on Augusta Avenue for a glass of wine, a game of klaberjass, pinochle, dominoes: she's happy he's enjoying himself. She blesses him on his way out. "God keep you in good health and return you in good health."

But when he is home of an evening reading the newspaper and comes across an item that engages his interest, he lets her in on it too. He shows her a picture of the Dionne quintuplets and explains exactly what happened out there in Callander, Ontario. This is a golden moment for her—she and Pa sitting over a newspaper discussing world events. Another time he shows her a picture of the Irish Sweepstakes winner. He won a hundred and fifty thousand, he tells her. She's entranced. *Mmm-mm-mm!* What she couldn't do with that money. They'd fix up the bathroom, paint the kitchen, clean out the backyard. *Mmm-mm-mm!* Pa says if we had that kind of money we could afford to put a match to a hundred-dollar bill, set fire to the house and buy a new one. She laughs at his wit. He's so clever, Pa.

Christmas morning King George VI is speaking on the radio. She's rattling around in the kitchen, Pa calls her to come and hear the King of England. She doesn't understand a word of English, but pulls up a chair and sits listening. "He stutters," says Pa. This she won't believe. A king? Stutters? But if Pa says so, it must be true. She bends an ear to the radio. Next day she has something to report to Mrs. Oxenberg, our next-door neighbour.

I speak of Pa's impatience with her; I get impatient with her too. I'm always at her about one thing and another, chiefly about the weight she's putting on. Why doesn't she cut down on the bread, does she have to drink twenty glasses of tea a day? No wonder her feet are sore, carrying all that weight. (My ma's a short woman a little over five feet and weighs almost two hundred pounds.) "Go ahead, keep getting fatter," I tell her. "The way you're going you'll never be able to get into a decent dress again."

But it's Pa who finds a dress to fit her, a Martha Washington Cotton size 52, which but for the length is perfect for her. He finds a shoe she can wear, Romeo Slippers with elasticized sides. And it's Pa who gets her to soak her feet, then sits with them in his lap scraping away with a razor blade at the calluses and corns.

Ma is my father's second wife, and our stepmother. My father, now sixty-three, was widowed thirty years ago. My sister was six at the time, I was five and my brother four when our mother died giving birth to a fourth child who lived only a few days. We were shunted around from one family to another who took us in out of compassion, till finally my father went to a marriage broker and put his case before him. He wanted a woman to make a home for his three orphans. An honest woman with a good heart, these were the two and only requirements. The marriage broker consulted his lists and said he thought he had two or three people who might fill the bill. Specifically, he had in mind a woman from Russia, roughly thirty years old, who was working without pay for relatives who had brought her over. She wasn't exactly an educated woman; in fact, she couldn't even read or write. As for honesty and heart, this he could vouch for. She was an orphan herself and as a child had been brought up in servitude.

Of the three women the marriage broker trotted out for him, my father chose Ma, and shortly afterward they were married.

* *

A COLOSTOMY. So it is cancer . . .

As of the second day Pa was in hospital I had taken to dropping in on him on my way home from work. "Nothing yet," he kept saying, "maybe tomorrow they'll find out."

After each of these visits, four in all, I reported to Ma that I had seen Pa. "He looks fine. Best thing in the world for him, a rest in the hospital."

"Pa's not lonesome for me?" she asked me once, and laughing, turned her head aside to hide her foolishness from me.

Yesterday Pa said to me, "It looks a little more serious than I thought. I have to have an operation tomorrow. Don't say anything to Ma. And don't come here for at least two or three days."

I take my time getting home. I'm not too anxious to face Ma—grinning like a monkey and lying to her the way I have been doing the last four days. I step into a hospital telephone booth to call my sister, Bella. She moans. "What are you going to say to Ma?" she asks.

I get home about half past six, and Ma's in the kitchen making a special treat for supper. A recipe given her by a neighbour and which she's recently put in her culinary inventory—pieces of cauliflower dipped in batter and fried in butter.

"I'm not hungry, Ma. I had something in the hospital cafeteria." (We speak in Yiddish; as I mentioned before, Ma can't speak English.)

She continues scraping away at the cauliflower stuck to the bottom of the pan. (Anything she puts in a pan sticks.)

107

"You saw Pa?" she asks without looking up. Suddenly she thrusts the pan aside. "The devil take it, I put in too much flour." She makes a pot of tea, and we sit at the kitchen table drinking it. To keep from facing her I drink mine leafing through a magazine. I can hear her sipping hers through a cube of sugar in her mouth. I can feel her eyes on me. Why doesn't she ask me, How's Pa? Why doesn't she speak? She never stops questioning me when I come from hospital, drives me crazy with the same questions again and again. I keep turning pages, she's still sucking away at that cube of sugar—a maddening habit of hers. I look up. Of course her eyes are fixed on me, probing, searching.

I lash out at her. "Why are you looking at me like that!"

Without answer she takes her tea and dashes it in the sink. She spits the cube of sugar from her mouth. (Thank God for that; she generally puts it back in the sugar bowl.)

She resumes her place, puts her hands in her lap and starts twirling her thumbs. No one in the world can twirl his thumbs as fast as Ma. When she gets them going they look like miniature windmills whirring around.

"She asks me why I'm looking at her like that," she says, addressing herself to the twirling thumbs in her lap. "I'm looking at her like that because I'm trying to read the expression in her face. She tells me Pa's fine, but my heart tells me different."

Suddenly she looks up, and thrusting her head forward, splays her hands out flat on the table. She has a dark-complexioned strong face, masculine almost, and eyes so black the pupil is indistinguishable from the iris.

"Do you know who Pa is!" she says. "Do you know who's lying in the hospital? I'll tell you who. The captain of our ship is lying in the hospital. The emperor of our domain. If the captain goes down, the ship goes with him. If the emperor leaves his throne, we can say good-bye to our domain. That's who's lying in the hospital. Now ask me why do I look at you like that."

She breaks my heart. I want to put my arms around her, but I can't do it. We're not a demonstrative family, we never kiss, we seldom show affection. We're always hollering at each other. Less than a month ago I hollered at Pa. He had taken to dosing himself. He was forever mixing something in a glass, and I became irritated at the powders, pills and potions lying around in every corner of the house like mouse droppings.

"You're getting to be a hypochondriac!" I hollered at him, not knowing what trouble he was in.

I reach out and put my hand over hers. "I wouldn't lie to you, Ma. Pa's fine, honest to God."

She holds her hand still a few seconds, then eases it from under and puts it over mine. I can feel the weight of her hand pinioning mine to the table, and in an unaccustomed gesture of tenderness we sit a moment with locked hands.

"You know I had a dream about Pa last night?" she says. "I dreamt he came home with a basket of apples. I think that's a good dream?"

MA'S IMMIGRATION TO CANADA had been sponsored by her Uncle Yankev. Yankev at the time he sent for his niece was in his mid-forties and had been settled a number of years in Toronto with his wife, Henye, and their five children. They made an odd pair, Yankev and Henye. He was a tall, 250-pound handsome man, and Henye was a lacklustre little woman with a pockmarked face, weighing maybe ninety pounds. Yankev was constantly abusing her. Old Devil, he called her to her face and in the presence of company.

Ma stayed three years with Yankev and his family, working like a skivvy for them and without pay. Why would Yankev pay his niece like a common servant? She was one of the family, she sat at table with them and ate as much as she wanted. She had a bed and even a room to herself, which she'd never had before. When Yankev took his family for a ride in the car to Sunnyside, she was included. When he bought ice-cream cones, he bought for all.

She came to Pa without a dime in her pocket.

Ma has a slew of relatives, most of them emigres from a remote little village somewhere in the depths of Russia. They're a crude lot, loudmouthed and coarse, and my father (but for a few exceptions) had no use for any of them. The Russian Hordes, he called them. He was never rude; anytime they came around to visit he simply made himself scarce.

One night I remember in particular; I must have been about seven. Ma was washing up after supper and Pa was reading a newspaper when Yankev arrived, with Henye trailing him. Pa folded his paper, excused himself, and was gone. The minute Pa was gone Yankev went to the stove and lifted the lids from the two pots. Just as he thought — *mamaliga* in one pot, in the other one beans, and in the frying pan a piece of meat their cat would turn its nose up at. He sat himself in the rocking chair he had given Ma as a wedding present, and rocking, proceeded to lecture her. He had warned her against the marriage, but if she was satisfied, he was content. One question and that's all. How had she bettered her lot? True, she was no longer an old maid. True, she was now mistress of her own home. He looked around him and snorted. A hovel. "And three snot-nose kids," he said, pointing to us.

Henye, hunched over in a kitchen chair, her feet barely reaching the floor, said something to him in Russian, cautioning him, I think. He told her to shut up, and in Yiddish continued his tirade against Ma. He had one word to say to her. To *watch* herself. Against his advice she had married this no-good Rumanian twister, this murderer. The story of how he had kept his first wife pregnant all the time was now well known. Also well known was the story of how she had died in her ninth month with a fourth child. Over an ironing board. Ironing his shirts while he was out playing cards with his Rumanian cronies and drinking wine. He had buried one wife, and now was after burying a second. So Ma had better watch herself, that's all.

Ma left her dishwashing and with dripping, wet hands took hold of a chair and seated herself facing Yankev. She begged him not to say another word. "Not another word, Uncle Yankev, I beg you. Till the day I die I'll be grateful to you for bringing me over. I don't know how much money you laid out for my passage, but I tried my best to make up for it the three years I stayed with you, by helping out in the house. But maybe I'm still in your debt? Is this what gives you the right to talk against my husband?"

Yankev, rocking, turned up his eyes and groaned. "You speak to her," he said to Henye. "It's impossible for a human being to get through to her."

Henye knew better than to open her mouth.

"Uncle Yankev," Ma continued, "every word you speak against my husband is like a knife stab in my heart." She leaned forward, thumbs whirring away. "*Mamaliga*? Beans? A piece of meat your cat wouldn't eat? A crust of bread at his board, and I will still thank God every day of my life that he chose me from the other two the *shadchan* showed him."

IN THE BEGINNING my father gave her a hard time. I remember his bursts of temper at her rough ways in the kitchen. She never opened a kitchen drawer without wrestling it—wrenching it open, slamming it shut. She never put a kettle on the stove without it running over at the boil. A pot never came to stove without its lid being inverted, and this for some reason maddened him. He'd right the lid, sometimes scalding his fingers—and all hell would break loose. We never sat down to a set or laid table. As she had been used to doing, so she continued; slamming a pot down on the table, scattering a handful of cutlery, dealing out assorted-size plates. More than once with one swipe of his hand my father would send a few plates crashing to the floor and stalk out. She'd sit a minute looking in our faces, one by one, then start twirling her thumbs and talking to herself. What had she done now?

"Eat!" she'd admonish us, and leaving table would go to the mirror over the kitchen sink and ask herself face to face, "What did I do now?" She would examine her face profile and front and then sit down to eat. After, she'd gather up the dishes, dump them in the sink, and running the water over them, would study herself in the mirror. "He'll be better," she'd tell herself, smiling. "He'll be soft as butter when he comes home. You'll see," she'd promise her image in the mirror.

Later in life, mellowed by the years perhaps (or just plain defeated—there was no changing her), he became more tolerant of her ways and was kinder to her. When it became difficult for her to get around because of her poor feet, he did her marketing. He attended to her feet, bought her the Martha Washingtons, the Romeo Slippers, and on a summer's evening on his way home from work, a brick of ice cream. She was very fond of it.

Three years ago he began promoting a plan, a plan to give Ma some pleasure. (This was during Exhibition time.) "You know," he said to me, "it would be very nice if Ma could see the fireworks at the Exhibition. She's never seen anything like that in her life. Why don't you take her?"

The idea of Ma going to the Ex for the fireworks was so preposterous, it made me laugh. She never went anywhere.

"Don't laugh," he said. "It wouldn't hurt you to give her a little pleasure once in a while."

He was quite keen that she should go, and the following

113

year he canvassed the idea again. He put money on the table for taxi and grandstand seats. "Take her," he said.

"Why don't you take her?" I said. "She'll enjoy it more going with you."

"Me? What will I do at the Exhibition?"

As children, we were terrified of Pa's temper. Once in a while he'd belt us around, and we were scared that he might take the strap to Ma too. But before long we came to know that she was the only one of us not scared of Pa when he got mad. Not even from the beginning when he used to let fly at her was she intimidated by him, not in the least, and in later years was even capable of getting her own back by taking a little dig at him now and then about the "aristocracy"—as she called my father's Rumanian connections.

Aside from his buddies in the back room of the ice-cream parlour on Augusta Avenue, my father also kept in touch with his Rumanian compatriots (all of whom had prospered), and would once in a while go to them for an evening. We were never invited, nor did they come to us. This may have been my father's doing, I don't know. I expect he was ashamed of his circumstances, possibly of Ma, and certainly of how we lived.

Once in a blue moon during Rosh Hashanah or Yom Kippur after shul, they would unexpectedly drop in on us. One time a group of four came to the house, and I remember Pa darting around like a gadfly, collecting glasses, wiping them, and pouring a glass of wine he'd made himself. Ma shook hands all around, then went to the kitchen to cut some slices of her honey cake, scraping off the burnt part. I was summoned to take the plate in to "Pa's gentle folk." Pretending to be busy, she rattled around the kitchen a few seconds, then seated herself in the partially open door, inspecting them. Not till they were leaving did she come out again, to wish them a good year.

The minute they were gone, my father turned on her. "Russian peasant! Tartar savage, you! Sitting there with your eyes popping out. Do you think they couldn't see you?"

"What's the matter? Even a cat may look at a king," she said blandly.

"Why didn't you come out instead of sitting there like a caged animal?"

"Because I didn't want to shame you," she said, twirling her thumbs and swaying back and forth in the chair Yankev had given her as a wedding present.

My father busied himself clearing table, and after a while he softened. But she wasn't through yet. "Which one was Falik's wife?" she asked in seeming innocence. "The one with the beard?"

This drew his fire again. "No!" he shouted.

"Oh, the other one. The pale one with the hump on her back," she said wickedly.

So . . . NOTWITHSTANDING the good dream Ma had of Pa coming home with a basket of apples, she never saw him again. He died six days after the operation.

It was a harrowing six days, dreadful. As Pa got weaker,

115

the more disputatious we became—my brother, my sister and I—arguing and snapping at each other outside his door, the point of contention being should Ma be told or not.

Nurse Brown, the special we'd put on duty, came out once to hush us. "You're not helping him by arguing like this. He can hear you."

"Is he conscious, nurse?"

"Of course he's conscious."

"Is there any hope?"

"There's always hope," she said. "I've been on cases like this before, and I've seen them rally."

We went our separate ways, clinging to the thread of hope she'd given us.

The fifth day after the operation I had a call from Nurse Brown: "Your father wants to see you."

Nurse Brown left the room when I arrived, and my father motioned me to undo the zipper of his oxygen tent. "Ma's a good woman," he said, his voice so weak I had to lean close to hear him. "You'll look after her? Don't put her aside. Don't forget about her—"

"What are you talking about!" I said shrilly, then lowered my voice to a whisper. "The doctor told me you're getting better. Honest to God, Pa, I wouldn't lie to you," I whispered.

He went on as if I hadn't spoken. "Even a servant if you had her for thirty years, you wouldn't put aside because you don't need her anymore—"

"Wait a minute," I said and went to the corridor to fetch Nurse Brown. "Nurse Brown, will you tell my father what you told me yesterday. You remember? About being on cases like this before, and you've seen them rally. Will you tell that to my father, please. He talks as if he's—"

I ran from the room and stood outside the door, bawling. Nurse Brown opened the door a crack. "Ssh! You'd better go now. I'll call you if there's any change."

At five the next morning my brother telephoned from hospital. Ma was sound asleep and didn't hear. "You'd better get down here," he said. "I think the old man's checking out. I've already phoned Bella."

My sister and I arrived at the hospital within seconds of each other. My brother was just emerging from Pa's room. In the gesture of a baseball umpire he jerked a thumb over his shoulder, signifying OUT.

"Is he dead?" we asked our brother.

"Just this minute," he replied.

Like three dummies we paced the dimly lit corridor, not speaking to each other. In the end we were obliged to speak; we had to come to a decision about how to proceed next.

We taxied to the synagogue of which Pa was a member, and roused the *shamus*. "As soon as it's light I'll get the rabbi," he said. "He'll attend to everything. Meantime, go home."

In silence we slowly walked home. Dawn was just breaking, and Ma, a habitually early riser, was bound to be up now and in the kitchen. Quietly we let ourselves in and passed through the hall leading to the kitchen. We were granted an unexpected respite; Ma was not yet up.

We waited ten minutes for her, fifteen—an agonizing wait. We decided one of us had better go and wake her; what was the sense in prolonging it? The next minute we changed our minds. To awaken her with such tidings would be inhuman, a brutal thing to do.

"Let's stop whispering," my sister whispered. "Let's talk in normal tones, do something, make a noise, she'll hear us and come out."

In an access of activity we busied ourselves. My sister put the kettle on with a clatter; I took teaspoons from the drawer, clacking them like castanets. She was bound to hear, their bedroom was on the same floor at the front of the house—but five minutes elapsed and not a sound from the room.

"Go and see," my sister said, and I went and opened the door to that untidy bedroom Pa used to rail against.

Ma, her black eyes circled and her hair in disarray, was sitting up in bed. At sight of me she flopped back and pulled the feather tick over her head. I approached the bed and took the covers from her face. "Ma—"

She sat up. "You are guests in my house now?"

For the moment I didn't understand. I didn't know the meaning of her words. But the next minute the meaning of them was clear—with Pa dead, the link was broken. The bond, the tie that held us together. We were no longer her children. We were now guests in her house.

"When did Pa die?" she asked.

"How did you know?"

"My heart told me."

Barefooted, she followed me to the kitchen. My sister gave her a glass of tea, and we stood like mutes, watching her sipping it through a cube of sugar.

"You were all there when Pa died?"

"Just me, Ma," my brother said.

She nodded. "His *kaddish*. Good."

I took a chair beside her, and for once without constraint or self-consciousness, put my arm around her and kissed her on the cheek.

"Ma, the last words Pa spoke were about you. He said you were a good woman. 'Ma's a good woman,' that's what he said to me."

She put her tea down and looked me in the face. "Pa said that? He said I was a good woman?" She clasped her hands. "May the light shine on him in paradise," she said, and wept silently, putting her head down to hide her tears.

Eight o'clock the rabbi telephoned. Pa was now at the funeral parlour on College near Augusta, and the funeral was to be at eleven o'clock. Ma went to ready herself, and in a few minutes called me to come and zip up her black crepe, the dress Pa had bought her six years ago for the Applebaum wedding.

The Applebaums, neighbours, had invited Ma and Pa to the wedding of their daughter, Lily. Right away Pa had declared he wouldn't go. Ma kept coaxing. How would it look? It would be construed as unfriendly, unneighbourly. A few days before the wedding he gave in, and Ma began scratching through her wardrobe for something suitable to wear. Nothing she exhibited pleased him. He went downtown and came back with the black crepe and an outsize corset.

I dressed her for the wedding, combed her hair and put some powder on her face. Pa became impatient; he had already called a cab. What was I doing? Getting her ready for a beauty contest? The taxi came, and as Pa held her coat he said to me in English, "You know, Ma's not a bad-looking woman?"

For weeks she talked about the good time she'd had at the Applebaum wedding, but chiefly about how Pa had attended her. Not for a minute had he left her side. Two hundred people at the wedding and not one woman among them had the attention from her husband that she had had from Pa. "Pa's a gentleman," she said to me, proud as proud.

Word of Pa's death got around quickly, and by nine in the morning people began trickling in. First arrivals were Yankev and his second wife. Yankev, now in his seventies and white-haired, was still straight and handsome. The same Yankev except for the white hair and an asthmatic condition causing him to wheeze and gasp for breath. He held out a hand to Ma, and with the other one thumped his chest, signifying he was too congested to speak.

From then on there was a steady influx of people. Here was Chaim the Schnorrer! We hadn't seen him in years. Chaim the Schnorrer, stinking of fish and in leg wrappings as always, instead of socks. Rich as Croesus he was said to be, a fish-peddling miser who lived on soda crackers and milk and kept his money in his leg wrappings. Yankev, a minute ago too congested for speech, found words for

Chaim. "How much money have you got in those *gutkes*? The truth, Chaim!"

Ma shook hands with all, acknowledged their sympathy, and to some she spoke a few words. I observed the Widow Spector, a gossip and trouble-maker, sidling through the crowd and easing her way towards Ma. "The Post" she was called by people on the street. No one had the time of day for her; even Ma used to hide from her.

I groaned at the sight of her. As if Ma didn't have enough to contend with. But no! here was Ma welcoming the Widow Spector, holding a hand out to her. "Give me your hand, Mrs. Spector. Shake hands, we're partners now. Now I know the taste, I'm a widow too." Ma patted the chair beside her. "Sit down, partner. Sit down."

At a quarter to eleven the house was clear of people. "Is it time?" Ma asked, and we answered, Yes, it was time to go. We were afraid this would be the breaking point for her, but she went calmly to the bedroom and took her coat from the peg on the door and came to the kitchen with it, requesting that it be brushed off.

The small funeral parlour was jammed to the doors, every seat taken but for four up front left vacant for us. On a trestle table directly in front of our seating was the coffin. A pine box draped in a black cloth, and in its centre a white Star of David.

Ma left her place, approached the coffin, and as she stood before it with clasped hands I noticed the uneven hemline of her coat, hiked up in back by that mound of flesh on her shoulders. I observed that her lisle stockings

121

were twisted at the ankles, and was embarrassed for her.

She stood silently a moment, then began to speak. She called him her dove, her comrade, her friend.

"Life is a dream," she said. "You were my treasure. You were the light of my eyes. I thought to live my days out with you—and look what it has come to." (She swayed slightly, the black shawl slipping from her head—and I observed that could have done with a brushing too.) "If ever I offended you or caused you even a twinge of discomfort, forgive me for it. As your wife I lived like a queen. Look at me now. I'm nothing. You were my jewel, my crown. With you at its head my house was a palace. I return now to a hovel. Forgive me for everything, my dove. Forgive me."

("Russian peasant," Pa used to say to her in anger, "Tartar savage." If he could see her now as she stood before his bier mourning him. Mourning him like Hecuba mourning Priam and the fall of Troy. And I a minute ago was ashamed of her hiked-up coat, her twisted stockings and dusty shawl.)

People were weeping; Ma resumed her place dry-eyed, and the rabbi began the service.

It is now a year since Pa died, and as he had enjoined me to do, I am looking after Ma. I have not put her aside. I get cross and holler at her as I always have done, but she allows for my testiness and does not hold it against me. I get bored telling her again and again that Pa's last words were "Ma's a good woman," and sometimes wish I'd never mentioned it. She cries a lot, and I get impatient with her tears. But I'm good to her.

This afternoon I called Moodey's, booked two seats for the grandstand, and tonight I'm taking her to the Ex and she'll see the fireworks.

The Apple Doesn't Fall
Far From the Tree

I MET LOTTIE KOGAN my first day in grade seven at King Edward Public School. It turned out that she and I lived on the same street, and overnight we became bosom pals. Lottie used to call for me every morning at a quarter to nine, but one morning she didn't show up and I was almost late for school. "I'll tell you later," she said when I asked her about it at recess. She then left the schoolyard, which was forbidden, raced across the street, and came back with a nickel bag of broken biscuits and licorice all-sorts, which she shared with me. She didn't call for me the next day, or the day after, but each time she had a nickel to spend at recess.

"Either you tell me why you stopped calling for me or I won't talk to you again."

"I can't call for you because I make a nickel on my way to school."

If she made a nickel on the way to school, why couldn't I? "Okay," she said, "but you'll have to be ready tomorrow at a quarter past eight sharp."

The next morning, instead of our usual route, we took

a detour by way of Carlyle Street where some excavation work was going on. A deep pit had been dug in the road, which was closed off to traffic, and a plank about fifteen feet long had been placed across the hole in which men were working.

"Watch me," said Lottie, "then do the same and you'll get a nickel."

She stepped out on the plank and slowly, sinuously, walked the length of it, sashaying and swinging her hips. At the other end she squatted, and peering into the pit, she held out her hand. Then she straightened out and beckoned me to follow.

I stepped out as she had done, sashaying and swinging my hips. When I was halfway across, a hand shot out and grabbed me by the inside of my thigh. I let out a shriek and ran to the other side. A man's head emerged from the pit, a scowl on the face. The man's hand came over the dugout, and Lottie took the nickel for me.

"Don't bring her here no more," he said to Lottie. "And don't you come back here neither."

Shortly after that, a new source of revenue opened up to us. Charlie Reilly, who worked as a teller in a bank, rented a room at the Kogans. He kept his room neat and paid his rent on time, always thanking Lottie's mother when he gave her the money. His room was next to the one Lottie shared with her sister, Jenny. (Jenny was two years older than Lottie, and wasn't all there.) Some evenings when Lottie and I went up to her room to do homework, Charlie would be lying spreadeagled on his bed, fully clothed, with a checkerboard across his chest. One night as we were passing he fired a couple of checkers at us. We picked them up and fired them back, and that was the beginning of the Checker Game.

Lottie and I would take a handful of checkers from the board on his chest, and positioning ourselves at the door, would take turns firing them as he lay there, arms flung wide and legs apart. Anytime it happened that we hit him in the groin, he would draw his knees up to his chest, squeal with pleasure, then spread himself wide again, inviting the next barrage. We knew it was a dirty game and that we risked being caught by Mrs. Kogan, who had called up one night asking what the racket was about. After that scare, Lottie shrewdly appraised the pros and cons of continuing to play the Checker Game.

"He gets a bang out of it," she said, "but what do we get?"

So Lottie put it to Charlie that we wouldn't play the Checker Game anymore unless there was something in it for us. She proposed that each of us would take the same number of checkers and take turns firing them. "You'll have to pay a dime to whoever gets the most hits," she told him, "and a nickel to the loser. Okay, Charlie?" And he agreed.

About two weeks after Lottie had put the Checker Game on a paying basis, Charlie was transferred to an outlying branch of the bank. He was sorry to leave, and we were sorry to see him go.

It was about this time that a scandal broke out on our street, a scandal involving Lottie's mother and a man called Tzarik. We were almost thirteen when Lottie's father went into partnership with Tzarik. Tzarik was a dark-complexioned, slow-moving, handsome man about twice the size of Lottie's father. The two of them would go to the country twice a week and bring back a truckload of live poultry. They would park the cackling fowl in front of Kogan's while Mrs. Kogan attended them, feeding them before market. The partnership lasted a few months and ended in a fight with Tzarik being thrown out of the house.

I was asleep when the fight broke out across the street, and it was my mother who said to me the next morning, "You didn't hear nothing? Kogan kicked his partner out of the house and the whole street came out, there was such a commotion. Mrs. Kogan was on the verandah crying and when she tried to go back in the house Kogan wouldn't let her come in. Mrs. Zaretsky, the grocer's wife, she said Kogan made his wife stay the whole night on the verandah before he let her come back in the house in the morning. When you finish your breakfast, go ask your friend what happened last night."

That morning I asked Lottie on our way to school, "What happened last night? My mother says your father kicked out Tzarik?"

"Tzarik's been crooking my father so he kicked him out."

But Mrs. Zaretsky told my mother: "Kogan found Tzarik fooling around with his wife. That's why he kicked him out."

**

128

LOTTIE BLOSSOMED the year we became thirteen. At recess she was no longer content to walk the schoolyard arm in arm with me, but was hankering now to be at the wire fence that separated the girls from the boys. We still walked arm in arm but she managed always to steer our course over to the fence.

These sessions were an abomination to me. I had no confidence in my looks. I was shy and leery of boys. But there we stood during recess, me with my head down and my best friend posing and prancing before the boys who were hanging over the fence.

Towards the end of the term a new girl was introduced into our class. One day at recess I saw her standing by herself. "Let's go over and talk to her," I said to Lottie. "She's new, she doesn't know anyone."

Lottie agreed and instead of going to the boys we went over to the new girl, Helen Loftus. Helen turned out to be every bit as boy-crazy as Lottie; she couldn't wait to get to the fence.

Before long it became apparent that Lottie preferred Helen's company to mine. I became moody and jealous.

"I don't know what's come over you," Lottie said to me one morning on our way to school. "You're getting to be a real pain in the neck."

After that year my friendship with Lottie began petering out. I used to see Helen and Lottie on the street, seldom one without the other. We would wave and on occasion stop to speak. I had no thought of renewing our friendship, but things fell otherwise.

Years later—we were both twenty—Lottie stopped me on the street to show me the diamond ring she was wearing. "I hope you'll come to my wedding," she said. "I've got you on my list."

I had heard she was engaged. Mrs. Stork, Dave's mother, told my mother, who told me, that Dave had given Lottie a diamond ring.

"Only one short month ago that they met," said Mrs. Stork. "And now the daughter of that *shikker* Kogan, his daughter is wearing my Dave's ring and a date for the wedding is already settled."

The Storks also lived on our street. Once or twice a week Mrs. Stork, a short woman with rosy cheeks, lively eyes and thick black hair showing a few strands of grey, would drop in to pass an hour or two with my mother.

Dave was Mr. and Mrs. Stork's only son. Their other two children were middle-aged twin daughters. Dave was born twenty years after the twins.

Mrs. Stork told my mother that Dave's birth had caused a stir in the street. He was born at home and as soon as word of the birth got around, the lying-in room was inundated. The mother, whom the women expected to find at least a little embarrassed, received them with unblushing smiles. She spoke of the baby as her "surprise baby."

"Surprise baby," said Mrs. Zaretsky, the grocer's wife. "It's a change-of-life baby. I would be ashamed to show my face."

Though the Storks lived only three doors away from us, I had had no contact with Dave. It was only when I went to work as bookkeeper for Peerless Dress that I met him. He had been with the firm three years. He was about five-foot-eight with a dark complexion, black hair and light-brown eyes. He had a pleasant face and was good-natured and obliging.

Mrs. Stork was not pleased with her son's choice. "It's not for me to say anything," she said to my mother. "Dave after all is twenty-five, and if Kogan's daughter suits him, I have nothing to say." Having said her piece, she wiped her mouth with an open hand, a meaningful gesture, signifying that no word of criticism will issue from the wiped mouth.

Two months later Dave put a wedding ring on his bride's finger. Helen, dressed to the nines, was Lottie's matron of honour. Helen had been married three years to a bookmaker who was unable to attend the wedding: he was doing a short stint for parole violation.

Everything from the ceremony to the reception went well. The bride's father got drunk, but that did not come as a surprise to anyone.

Mrs. Kogan was dancing when she caught sight of her husband. "If there is any shame in you," she said to him, "you'll leave the hall right now, this minute, and go home before everyone here sees you in your wet pants."

The next day, and for many days following, the women on the street had something to talk about.

MR. YANOVSKY OWNED Peerless Dress and his business prospered. Extra sewing machines were installed, extra hands hired, among them a second shipper, Jack Kaminsky, recently arrived from Vancouver with his widowed mother. Thirty years old, overweight, average height, he was a man of beefy good looks with wavy brown hair and blue eyes.

"He's been here a couple of months now and hasn't made a single friend. I think the guy is lonely here in Toronto," Dave said one day. He took Jack home with him one night and introduced him to his wife. The three of them began going out together—to the movies, wrestling matches, bowling alleys, Chinatown, and later on to Dave's parents' for supper on Friday nights.

Once when she was visiting my mother, Mrs. Stork said to me, "Come to my house for supper tomorrow. Your mother told me your father is coming home—what does she need you? Come to my house for supper."

After being out of work a while, my father got a job in Kitchener with a friend who ran a large grocery store. My mother missed him, and when he phoned, which he did once a week, she'd hope he'd say he was coming home for the weekend. With my father home my mother had no need of me, or of anyone for that matter. Chances were that he'd be out playing cards with his cronies most of his homecoming weekend, but that didn't disturb my mother. The comforting thing was that Pa was home.

I accepted Mrs. Stork's invitation to supper.

"Jack's staying home, his mother is sick," Dave said when he and Lottie called for me.

The door to the living room was open and Mr. Stork, looking glum, was sitting in his chair; his paper lay by his feet, unopened. We walked down the hall to the kitchen.

Mrs. Stork was at the stove.

"What's the matter with Pa?" Dave asked. "Why's he wearing such a long face?"

"Maybe he got up on the wrong side," said Mrs. Stork. "Go in the parlour. In ten minutes supper will be ready."

When we went back to the living room Lottie went over to Mr. Stork and sat on his lap. "What's the matter, Pa?" she said. Nuzzling him, rubbing her cheek against his, Lottie wriggled and squirmed in his lap with her bare arms around his neck, till the man was in a visible sweat.

"Lottie!" Mrs. Stork called from across the room; she had been standing in the doorway. "Get down from Pa's lap, you're not a baby no more." A rush of angry blood had made her face red. She turned to me. "Come, you'll give me a hand in the kitchen.

"Sit," she said when we were in the kitchen. "I'll attend to everything my own self. Tell me, how come she didn't bring him tonight?"

"Who?" I said, knowing she meant Jack Kaminsky.

"Who? The *bik*," she said harshly. "They go everywhere together. What happened that she didn't bring him tonight? You're a smart woman. Say yourself, is this the way to treat a husband like Dave? A good provider, a kind man, an honest husband. Shouldn't she be ashamed? I would like to speak to her but my husband, he told me strictly I shouldn't say a word."

"You could be wrong, Mrs. Stork. I think Jack is just a good friend."

"A good friend—Lottie can be a good friend with a man! You saw the way she was sitting in Stork's lap. She knows what she was doing. Besides, that's an insult to me. I'm not such an old woman yet. Let's talk straight. The apple doesn't fall far from the tree. The mother was a *kurveh* and so is the daughter. Didn't the mother have another man? You were best friends with Lottie. You should remember Tzarik."

"Tzarik was Mr. Kogan's business partner," I said. "And the quarrel was about business. I remember the whole story."

She looked shrewdly at me. "Who said he wasn't a partner? He was a partner with everything. A partner with the business and a partner with the wife."

My HUSBAND and I were married at the City Hall, with a couple of strangers rustled up as witnesses. We lived in a furnished flat in a lovely old house on Avenue Road. Lottie and Dave had been married three years and a few months. I was still working for Peerless Dress. Dave and I got along well, we liked each other. Jack Kaminsky I saw once a week, on Wednesdays when he came to the office for his pay envelope. Without a word, a smile, a glance, he took his pay envelope from my hand as if from a vending machine. When Dave recommended a movie they'd seen, or a new Chinese restaurant they'd tried, I knew they were still going about together—Lottie, Dave and Jack.

One night when Dave was on the road we had a call from Lottie. She wanted to come over. "Do you mind if I bring a friend?"

The friend she brought was Jack Kaminsky.

It was hard work making conversation with him. My husband asked about Vancouver. What was the weather like? Jack said it was great for ducks. But the totem poles in Stanley Park, they were really something to see. Apart from the totem poles, he could think of nothing else about Vancouver that might be of interest. Decked out in a tan gabardine suit with a vest, teal-blue shirt with button-down collar, two-tone shoes, he sat like a stump, without saying a word.

Lottie called me aside as they were leaving. "Look, I'm not going home yet. Dave is supposed to be home around ten in the morning, but he could just change his schedule and get home around three or four, so I left a note saying I'm staying here overnight. Okay? I usually stay at my mother's when he goes out of town, but my mother and father and Jenny are in New York visiting my aunt. That's why I thought I'd better leave a note saying I'm staying here—just in case." Then she said, "If I'm trusting you this far, I might as well go all the way—we're having an affair."

"What if Dave does get home at three or four and phones here first thing in the morning and you're not here?" I asked.

"He won't phone you. When he gets in at three or four he always sleeps till noon. Anyway, I'll check with you in the morning."

Now that I was in her confidence, they never went to a hotel for the night without Lottie telephoning me first to establish an alibi. It worried me in the beginning. We weren't that close anymore, and Dave knew that.

"You don't have to worry about a thing," she said. "Do you think I'd leave him a note saying where I am? Give me credit for more sense. Dave knows I don't always sleep at home when he's out of town, but he never asks if I did or didn't. He takes it for granted that I sleep at my mother's. So far I haven't even used your name. I'm keeping it in reserve, is all. Just in case there's a slip-up and he gets to know that I didn't sleep at home or at my mother's, I've got you to fall back on." Apt in deceit, she left nothing to chance.

Lottie telephoned me one Saturday morning and invited me to lunch. "Things are getting serious," she said, "and I have to talk to someone."

I arrived at the restaurant, surprised at her having chosen such an expensive place; Lottie was close with money. We exchanged greetings, the waiter took our orders and Lottie got down to cases.

"Do you think it's possible to love two men at the same time?"

"I don't know. I can't speak from firsthand experience."

"Let's face it," she said, "I wasn't in love with Dave when I married him. I liked him, I liked him a lot. Now I've got two men on my hands and my feelings have changed. I think I'm beginning to feel something like love for him, believe it or not."

"Who? Which one?"

"Look, are you going to be serious or not? Jack keeps

bugging me to divorce Dave and marry him."

I didn't believe for a minute that she had any intention of divorcing Dave, the money-maker, to marry Jack, the no-account shipper. But I went along.

"What would you gain by divorcing Dave to marry Jack?"

"That's what I keep asking myself. In lots of ways I like Jack better than Dave. And Dave likes him too. The funny thing is the way they've become so palsy-walsy. They go to the ball games together, the fights, the hockey matches. And any time we decide to take in a movie Dave always says, 'Let's ask Jack.' So the three of us go to the movie, come back to our place for a bite to eat, and except for all of us getting in the same bed I might as well have two husbands." She sobered. "Give Dave a couple of years and he'll be a partner in the firm. Jack has no ambition, he'll be a shipper till he drops."

She finished her coffee, opened her handbag, put some powder on her face and applied fresh lipstick to her mouth. Her hair, worn short, was auburn, with a glossy sheen and a natural wave. She had large, dark-brown eyes and thick eyelashes. Despite a thin-lipped mouth, which gave a sly look to her face, she was undeniably attractive.

I was not persuaded that Jack wanted her to divorce Dave and marry him. He was dumb, but not so dumb that he didn't know clover when he was in it. Still, I don't think Lottie was telling an out-and-out lie. He probably had proposed that she divorce Dave and marry him. But as it was four years or better that they had been lovers, Jack would know by now the kind of woman he was dealing with. He wouldn't have to be too bright to know he wasn't sticking his neck out, proposing marriage.

I was proven wrong on both counts. Several months after I'd had lunch with Lottie, Jack phoned and asked me to meet him. He had something important to discuss. I agreed to meet him at ten o'clock at a restaurant a short distance from where I lived. When I arrived, he was sitting in a booth towards the back. I saw him as soon as I came in—I could hardly miss him, duded up as he was. He was wearing a fawn-and-blue plaid sports jacket, pink shirt, matching pocket handkerchief and mauve tie with purple dots. I sat down opposite him. He was freshly barbered and too strongly scented for ten in the morning.

He looked up from cutting his prune Danish. His hands were beefy, his fingers square, his fingernails none too clean.

"Hello there," he said, keeping his seat. "I really appreciate your coming. I'd like to ask you some personal questions. And I'll appreciate it if you'll tell me the truth without worrying about hurting my feelings."

"Go ahead."

"Would you call Lottie a sincere woman?"

"Sincere?"

"By that I mean honest."

"Honest?" I was puzzled.

"What I mean is, is Lottie a person you could trust to keep her word?"

"Well, that would depend of course on—"

138

He didn't wait to hear me out. He talked about his mother—a wonderful woman who had worked like a horse bringing up three small children after his father took off with another woman. The other two, his sisters, were married and living out west. He was the only one left, and owed his mother a debt he could never repay. He had told her about Lottie, but she was against it.

"What can you expect from an old-fashioned type like my mother? How would you expect her to react if her only son tells her that he's in love with a married woman?" He paused, as if waiting for an answer. "You couldn't expect her to jump from joy, could you?"

"No," I agreed.

But that wasn't his problem. The problem was Lottie. For almost five years they'd had an intimate relationship. Was she stringing him along? Or could she be trusted to keep her word about divorcing Dave to marry him?

"She keeps telling me to wait. How long can I wait? I'm not getting any younger. That's why I decided to talk to you. You've known Lottie about twelve or thirteen years. If any person can say that she's a woman you can trust to keep her word or not, that person is you. You know Lottie better than anybody does."

"When Lottie and I were close friends, we were just kids. It's only recently that we've been seeing each other again. If anyone knows Lottie, it's you. I'd say you know her better than even Dave does."

He gave me a sullen, ill-humoured look. "That's a shitty thing to say."

"You told me not to spare your feelings," I reminded him.

He got up. "Thanks for nothing." He stopped at the cashier's to pay for his Danish and left.

THE NEXT TIME I saw Lottie she was in hospital recuperating from an emergency operation. One morning she had woken with acute abdominal pains. An examination revealed an ectopic pregnancy. Infection had set in and a hysterectomy was performed.

"I'll never be able to have any kids," Lottie said. "But I'm not sorry about that. If I got pregnant I'd worry about having a kid that might turn out to be like Jenny. If that runs in the family, it could happen to me too."

Lottie thanked me for coming to visit her. "Dave said that you're leaving Peerless Dress? That you and your husband are going to Europe?"

"That's right. To London first, then to the continent for as long as our money holds out."

"Don't forget to send a card."

To use my mother's expression: the days are long and the years are short. Seven years went by. My marriage broke up. My father died. My mother is in a nursing home, grieving, desolate. She has become hard of hearing, her eyes have weakened; my father's death knocked the props from under her.

I visit her often. She blesses me when I arrive, blesses me when I leave. She asks about my husband. I tell her he's fine. Sends his regards. She doesn't know we've broken up.

Why burden her with my misadventure? She has enough on her plate.

One day when I was visiting her, she spoke sadly of past events, of Mrs. Kogan's death, assuming she'd already told me. Before I left, my mother told me that Mrs. Stork often came to visit her. I decided I would phone Mrs. Stork and thank her.

When I got home I called Lottie's number before calling Mrs. Stork. "Well, well, well," she said, "a voice from the past. How long is it anyway since the last time I saw you?"

"The last time was when I came to see you in the hospital. That would be about . . . seven years ago?"

"Could be."

"My mother told me that your mother died. I was very sorry to hear that, Lottie. When did it happen?"

"About a year now. She had a heart attack and died three days later in her sleep. If you've gotta go, that's the way to go. Poor Jenny, she's really heartbroken, you never saw anything like it. And my old man took it very hard too, believe it or not. By that I mean when he was sober enough to realize what had happened."

"How's Dave?"

"Fine. He's out of town at the moment with a new line. Say, if it's seven years that we saw you, you wouldn't have heard that Dave is a partner now with Yanovsky."

"Congratulations," I said. "I remember the day you predicted that Dave would be a partner."

"Did I? Hold the line a minute, someone's at the door

. . . It's Jack," she said, returning. "Would you like to say hello to him?"

"Give him my regards," I said. "I'll be seeing you, Lottie."

"Don't be a stranger," she said.

"Come over," Mrs. Stork said when I called to thank her. "I didn't see you for—I don't know myself how many years. Come over tomorrow."

Mrs. Stork had not changed much. Her hair had gone grey, but she was still a robust woman with rosy cheeks and lively eyes.

Mr. Stork was in the living room, listening to the radio. I would not have known him. He was diabetic and had changed beyond recognition.

Mrs. Stork and I went to the kitchen. She put homemade cookies on a plate and poured tea. We settled in for a talk.

"You saw Lottie lately?" she asked.

"I haven't seen her in years, but we spoke on the phone yesterday. She told me that Dave is a partner now with Yanovsky."

"What else did she tell you, the *nafka*?" she said, and we're off to the races.

"You're a clever woman—tell me, is my son blind? Is he blind that he can't see what's going on in front of his nose? You know how many years now that people are talking? Laughing at Dave? Twelve, thirteen years. Even Helen, she happened to be in the district, she said, so she thought she'd step in and say hello. To say hello—Helen, her best friend, she came specially to tell me that when Dave goes out of town they go everywhere together like a married couple, to a moving picture, to a restaurant, a beer parlour. When it comes to stabbing me in the heart they know where to find me, even Helen. I heard from somebody that Mrs. Zaretsky said that Dave acts like he's the *shadchan*, he's so happy about the whole thing. She said Dave doesn't care what his wife is doing because he's got a tootsie on the side. This I don't believe. Dave is an honest husband. Blind, yes. A fool, yes. But an honest husband. On Friday night when I see them here at my table, she in the middle, my son on one side, and on her other side the *bik*, my *kishkas* get tied up in knots. You know it's a sin to wish on somebody they should die—I have to bite my tongue not to wish him he should drop dead."

On a Sunday Dave telephoned with shocking news. It was not quite a year since I had spoken to Lottie and now she was dead. Dave and Jack were playing gin rummy after supper, and Lottie was washing up when suddenly they noticed that she was in some kind of trouble.

"She was standing at the sink," Dave said, "bent over and clutching her left breast, you could see she was in pain. Next minute she flakes out and she's on the floor, unconscious. I phoned a doctor, he took his time coming, the son of a bitch. Anyway, that didn't make any difference, she was dead about two minutes after she flaked out. Goddamn it! Lottie didn't waste no time checking out."

It was hot the day of the funeral. The atmosphere in the funeral parlour was stifling. Some people were seated, some were standing around talking, almost everyone wiping sweat from his face. It was one o'clock and the rabbi had not arrived.

The coffin, open, was on a stand at the front of the chapel. Jenny, whom I had last seen about fifteen years ago at Lottie's wedding, was standing near the coffin. But for an accumulation of flesh, Jenny did not look any different than she had fifteen years before.

I went up to her and held out my hand. "Remember me, Jenny? Lottie and I used to be friends when we went to King Edward, remember me?"

Holding my hand loosely in hers, she said, "You wanna see Lottie?" She pointed to the coffin.

They had put too much makeup on Lottie. Crimson lipstick thickly applied to her mouth had given a Cupid's-bow shape to her thin lips. Her hair was dyed a luminous copper, her eyelashes were thick with mascara, and her eyelids had royal-blue shadow on them. She looked awful.

I felt someone's hand on my shoulder. It was Dave. His head was partially covered by a *yarmulke*.

"They put too much makeup on her," he said, looking at Lottie. "She never used any of that crap. Used to touch up her hair is all."

Lottie's father came up and said something to Dave, something I didn't catch. His breath reeked. Dave took hold of his arm. "I'm warning you, Kogan," he said, his voice trembling, "you step out of line and I'll kick the living shit out of you."

Raising his hand, Kogan made a sort of conciliatory

144

gesture, turned and walked unsteadily down the aisle.

"He got drunk at his daughter's wedding," Dave said, watching him, "now he's getting drunk at her funeral. He's got a bottle on him. Give him half a chance and he'll turn Lottie's funeral into a sideshow. Nice seeing you again." He walked away.

Looking around I recognized people I had not seen in years. Customers, salesmen, Mr. Yanovsky and his wife, designers, cutters, pressers, operators, floor girls, finishers. Peerless Dress was well represented. Everyone liked Dave.

I saw Helen coming towards me. She was overdressed, in black.

"Hello there," she said to me. "I saw you looking at Lottie—what does she look like?"

"Go and see for yourself."

She put a black-gloved hand to her heart. "That's all I need now, to see a dead person. You know I never saw a dead person in my whole life? Here comes Jack." She whispered: "He looks terrible. Lottie's dying makes him a widower too, if you get my meaning . . . Hello, Jack," she said as he came up. "That was a terrible thing to happen. And to Lottie of all people. Look who's here," she said, presenting me.

"If you want to come out to the cemetery," he said, "I'm looking after the cars for Dave." He had put on a lot of weight. There was sweat on his face and his breath was bad. I thanked him and said I would not be going to the cemetery.

"See you," he said and left us.

"Boy oh boy," said Helen, "he acts like he's Dave's best friend. And Dave hasn't got a clue. Imagine outfoxing a sharp guy like Dave all these years. How did she ever get away with it!"

The rabbi walked up the aisle, put down the lid of the coffin and took his place at the lectern.

Helen put her arm through mine. "Let's sit together, us two, like in the old days. Out of respect for Lottie."

The rabbi started riffling through the pages of his prayer book. He put the open prayer book on the lectern and began the eulogy. He spoke well of Lottie, lauded her, praised her. He went on and on, overdoing it by far. At last he took up the open prayer book. "*Yiskadal v'yiskadash shmey raba*," he began, and we got to our feet.

WE WERE STANDING outside the nursing home, Mrs. Stork and I. She had been to visit my mother, and we stopped to talk. It was the evening after Lottie's funeral, and Mrs. Stork was telling me about how she'd gone to Dave's place, with food she'd prepared for the house of *shivah*. Dave, she said, was sitting on a small stool. The shocking thing was seeing Jack nearby, sitting on a crate. Both men were in stocking feet.

"A man cannot sit *shivah* for his *nafka*," she said harshly. "The husband, my Dave, he sits *shivah* for her."

She said when she got home and told Stork about it, he nearly fainted, a sick man. He got on the phone to Rabbi Isaacs.

"An old man, he's the rabbi of the *shul* we belong to. I

146

didn't hear what Stork said to him. But Stork told me that Rabbi Isaacs, he'll take care of everything."

That morning she arrived early at Dave's. When the rabbi came at ten o'clock, Mrs. Stork was already there.

"He came in, said *shalom*, didn't look even once on me, the old rabbi, he looked only on the two men sitting *shivah*. 'Which one is the husband?' he asked. My Dave said he was. 'And you,' the rabbi said to the *bik*, 'what were you to this man's wife—her father? Her brother?' He didn't answer, so Dave said, 'He's a good friend, Rabbi. He was also a good friend to my wife.'

"'You were not the husband,' the rabbi said to the *bik*, 'you were not the woman's father, and you were not her brother. The husband says you were a good friend to his wife, but that does not give you the right to sit *shivah* for her. So get up from that box, mister, and put on your shoes.'"

It's ONE YEAR since Lottie died, and one year that Jack has been sharing the apartment with Dave. The move was made after Lottie's funeral. It was the day Rabbi Isaacs came at ten in the morning and ordered Jack to get up from the crate and put on his shoes. According to Mrs. Stork, Jack obeyed the rabbi's order without question. He left the apartment, and whether it was at Dave's invitation or of his own volition, he returned an hour or so later with four packed cases and made himself at home. As for his mother, to whom he owed a debt he could never repay, he had left her, an eighty-five-year-old woman, to fend for herself.

Mrs. Stork telephoned. She calls me from time to time.

She told me again that her heart aches for Dave. Without Lottie he's lonesome. "To have the *bik* in the apartment, it's better for Dave than to be by himself," she said. "This way they play cards, go to a moving picture, a baseball game. And they talk about Lottie, what a wonderful woman she was. Thank God I took Stork's advice and didn't say nothing to Dave. It's better this way, that he doesn't know from anything. Lottie after all is dead, finished, kaput, a picnic for the worms. I feel pity for her too. I have to go now. Stork wants me. I'll phone you again, keep well."

I WENT BACK to the living room and poured myself another drink. Dave was still on his first. I offered to freshen it. "One's my limit," he said, "thanks just the same." I should know by now that he never accepts more than one drink.

Two months ago Dave began stopping off at my apartment once or twice a week, usually early in the evening on his way home from work. He accepts a drink when he comes, never more than one, and we talk. I should say it is Dave who talks. I listen, make a comment when it's called for. He usually stays an hour, during which time he talks of Lottie, of Jack, and of his and Lottie's friendship with Jack. He talks of nothing else. I like Dave, but his visits are trying. He wears me out, harping on the same theme. I can't tell whether he has belatedly become suspicious of his wife's relationship with Jack. So when he invites a comment, I don't know whether he's encouraging me to open up, suspecting perhaps that I know more than I'm

148

letting on. His visits have become a trial. It takes three or four whiskies to get me through the hour he puts in at my place.

"As I mentioned before," Dave said, "we talk a lot about Lottie. And lately he's been telling me that he was in love with her—as if I didn't know that. But I never worried about them being together when I was out of town, and that's the God's honest truth. When I'd come home from being on the road, Lottie would tell me the different places they'd been to. 'We always go Dutch,' she said. Which didn't surprise me. He's not the fastest guy in the world with a buck, you know." Dave looked at his watch and got up. "I'd better get going, he'll be phoning the hospitals."

One day last week Dave said, "Yesterday I got home later than usual and I could tell by the colour of his face that he'd been into the booze. That's one sign. Another sign is when he starts running off at the mouth. And sure enough, soon as I sat down he starts telling me that if he'd met Lottie first, I wouldn't of stood a chance with her.

"Me," Dave said, his thumb jabbing his chest, "I wouldn't of stood a chance with her, get that."

He paused to take a drink. "Lottie didn't mind him around. She liked him, but mostly she felt sorry for him. She used to say that his miserable childhood was responsible for his weak character."

Dave finished his drink and got up. "If he'd met her first—he talks such foolishness when he's tanked. Not that he's an Einstein when he's sober.

"He's getting to be a pain in the ass. I pay the rent,

149

hydro, telephone, the cleaning woman, he doesn't even chip in for the food. Never buys a bottle, he drinks my liquor, the free-loader. And that takes some nerve, don't you think?"

"I certainly do. Why do you put up with it, Dave?"

He shrugged. "I don't know. Habit, I guess. Used to having him around . . . He's got some filthy habits," Dave continued. "He's got an itchy back that he scratches with a fork. No kidding, when he feels an itch, he takes off his tie, unbuttons his shirt and goes to work on his bare back with a fork. And puts the fork back in the drawer without washing it. Another thing he does is he comes out of the toilet after he's had a crap—excuse my language—without washing his hands. And he sweats a lot. A person that sweats the way he does should take a bath every day instead of maybe once a week the way he does."

Dave came by yesterday and I got out the bottle. Before sitting down to his drink he took a small, unframed photo from his jacket pocket and showed it to me. It was a sidewalk photographer's photo of Dave and Lottie. "Remember this picture?" he said.

"I think so. But wasn't Jack in it too?"

When I'd seen it on Lottie's dresser, it had been a photo of the three of them, Lottie in the centre, Dave to one side of her and Jack on the other.

"You've got a good memory," said Dave. "Jack was in the picture."

He put the photo back in his pocket and sat down to his drink. Smiling, he said, "Yesterday when I happened to be looking at that picture, I thought to myself what a nice picture that would be of me and Lottie—if Jack wasn't in it. A pair of scissors happened to be handy and so I cut Jack out. It wasn't his picture anyway. He never paid for it, I did. He didn't see it till last night after supper. He blew his top when he saw it."

Dave laughed. "He said it was spite that made me cut him out of the picture. I was jealous, he said, because Lottie liked him. Me? Jealous of that slob because Lottie liked him?"

He took a long drink and put down his glass. "Lottie was a looker," he said. "Shit, if she wanted to play around— and she had plenty of opportunities with me out on the road—the last guy in the world she'd pick would be a fat guy who dresses like a fairy, douses himself with that whorish cologne, sweats like a pig, scratches his back with a fork, and comes out of the can without washing his hands."

Dave finished his drink and stood up. "She felt sorry for him is all."

Intercede for Us, Auntie Chayele

"LET'S HAVE A DRINK before the rest get here," said my brother, Aaron, and my sister, Bella, went to her cupboard for the bottle. Aaron poured us each a stiff shot of whisky and raised his glass. "*L'chaim,*" he said, and we drank.

My sister began to cry. "Poor Ma. I hope she didn't know she was dying. She was always so frightened of death."

Our stepmother, seventy-three, deaf and almost blind, had spent the last two years of her life in a nursing home. We had seen her only a few days before: she was in good health and it was a shock when they phoned from the nursing home and said she had had a stroke. She lived only two days without regaining consciousness, and now the three of us had come back from her funeral.

"How about Mischa taking a dive at the cemetery?" my brother said. "That guy should have been an actor instead of a hat manufacturer. And how about Gedalyeh? He cried enough for all."

My brother was talking of our stepmother's nephews, the brothers Gedalyeh and Mischa, sons of her only sister,

153

Genesha, who had been dead many years.

My sister, who was at the window on the lookout for the brothers, shrugged. "Hypocrites," she said. "Here they come."

Arm in arm the brothers came in, their wives behind them. Gedalyeh, fifty-three, the trucker, piloted his brother Mischa, forty-six, the hat manufacturer, to an easy chair.

"Give him a schnapps," he said to Aaron. "You know how he has a habit to faint when he feels bad."

Having settled his brother, Gedalyeh put his hands over his face and stood centre floor, immobilized. His wife, Ethel, a big woman and taller than Gedalyeh by half a head, took him by the arm and guided him to a chair. She broke open a packet of pocket-size Kleenex and stood over him, handing him piece by piece.

"This is a terrible shock to him," she said. "I don't have to tell you how much he loved his Auntie Chayele. And I know you three kids feel just as bad even if you don't show it so much. After all, what mother did you know except her? You were little kids when your own mother died, babies. Your father, may he rest in peace, had a hard time to make a living, but she gave him all the respect in the world and brought you up like her own children."

Ethel was a simple woman, kind-hearted and sincere. Everything she spoke she meant.

Gedalyeh, with tears to spare, began crying all over again.

"Intercede for us, Auntie Chayele," he intoned, going into Yiddish. "Intercede for us in Paradise where you've earned your rightful place. Intercede for your worthless nephews, Gedalyeh and Mischa. Intercede for their wives, my two children, and also for the three orphans you brought up."

There was a litter of sodden Kleenex at Gedalyeh's feet. I saw my sister's eye on it as he kept dropping it piece by piece to the floor. Mischa's wife, Flo, had positioned herself on the arm of her husband's chair. She kept scrutinizing him, worried that he might faint again.

Mischa had come up in the world since the day we first saw him. It was twenty-four years ago when Mischa, a greenhorn of twenty-two in an electric-blue suit short in the pants, arrived from Chileshea, a remote little village somewhere in the depths of Russia. Gedalyeh brought him to our house and I remember how Ma wept with joy over the nephew whom she'd last seen as a little boy, then with bitter tears for her sister, Genesha, of whose death she'd had no knowledge till Mischa's arrival. She couldn't get her fill of Mischa, and when it came time to go home she begged Gedalyeh to let him stay with us.

"Where will you put him?" she said. "You're already sleeping three in a room and Ethel is going to have another baby any day."

Gedalyeh, who had preceded his brother in immigration by several years, was already a married man with a child and another one on the way. He conceded his Auntie Chayele was right. He embraced his brother and kissed him on the mouth and went home to Ethel.

Mischa talked for hours after his brother left, and Ma,

155

remembering her own experience when she had emigrated seventeen years before, kept moaning in sympathy as he recounted his fright on embarkation, the dreadful crossing, and his bewilderment on arrival with only four words of the language—Hello, Good-bye, Please and Tenk you.

My father came from work and shook hands with Mischa, giving him a sideways look. A whole tribe of Ma's relatives had settled in Toronto, most of them from Chileshea, and but for a few exceptions, he had very little use for any of them. The Russian Hordes, he called them. They, in turn, jeered behind his back. The Rumanian Beast, he was called—or the Mamaliga Eater.

Ma went to the kitchen to prepare supper. She made a great clatter, as always, then stood in the open door signalling Pa. "I want him to stay here," she said in Yiddish, and in a whisper all could hear. Seventeen years she had been in the land, sixteen of them married to Pa, who spoke English well, but not a word had she learned. In the house we always spoke Yiddish.

"My sister died," she continued in a whisper. "He's an orphan. I want him to stay here, it will ease my heart."

And my father couldn't say no to her. In the sixteen years they had been married she had never asked anything of him, certainly never anything for herself. My father was a luckless man scratching all his life for a living. He worked his heart out on whatever job he undertook but misfortune followed him like a shadow. But Ma loved him and cherished him; and so long as it was at his hands, was content with whatever fell to her lot. Only God knows why, but she counted herself the luckiest woman in the land the day that Pa, an impoverished widower with three small orphans, selected her from the three candidates the marriage broker had canvassed.

News of Mischa's arrival made the rounds and a week of merry-making was given over in celebration of it. They were a crude lot, the Chilesheans, and the gatherings were noisy, ribald. The nicknames they tagged each other with were malicious, wicked—but a kind of tribal solidarity did exist among them and everyone was eager to give the orphaned greenhorn a leg-up. Yitzhok Gruber, called behind his back The Ape, offered Mischa a job in his bicycle parts repair shop. Raisel the Galloping Consumptive wanted him to come into her hand laundry. "Stay away from her," Mischa was warned. "Six months ago the rabbi gave her a divorce because she claimed her husband was a eunuch. She's hungry, she'll eat you up, a good-looking boy." Zosia Crooked-Ass had a place for him in his grocery store. And so it went. Genesha's orphan was the darling of the moment. Later he became known as Mischa Liar.

In three weeks Mischa was working for a hat factory, apprenticed to a blocker, and at night was going to school for English. In six months he was speaking reasonably well; but so scrupulous, so overzealous had he been in avoiding the common errors in pronunciation—like pronouncing the *th* sound as *t*—that at the end of the course he was speaking a very peculiar English indeed. Table became *thable*, talk became *thalk*, take became *thake*, and so on.

In three years he had a bank account and a diamond

ring and was dating a girl called Bessie whom he'd met at Sunnyside in a public dancing casino. And the liar he had become! The lies he told were purposeless, seldom anything to further his advantage or to get him out of a scrape: he was simply a compulsive chronic liar. He was leery of the truth, he didn't trust it, and it was virtually impossible for him to speak it. In less than a year he was being called Mischa Liar, even by his brother, Gedalyeh. The first few times he was caught out he would get a nose bleed or go into a faint. But later with money in the bank to bolster his confidence, he was able to brazen it out and his nose bled only on occasion.

Ma adored him, she forgave him everything. So he had told a little lie, what harm was there? Did he rob, cheat, kill? No fixed amount had ever been set for Mischa's board and lodging, and the first six months she took nothing from him. "An extra mouth, what does it come to?" Later, when he was earning at least three times as much as my father, he would slip her a few dollars. Always she protested, sometimes putting it back in his pocket. . . . "Keep it, you'll need it for yourself, a young boy starting out in the world."

Mischa stayed with us three years, and when he was twenty-five he moved to a bachelor apartment. The leave-taking was very dramatic. His nose bled when he kissed his Auntie Chayele good-bye. When he shook hands with Pa he had to sit down to keep from fainting.

He came to us Friday nights for supper, and one Friday announced his intention of getting married to Bessie, the dance hall lady whom we'd never met. An engagement party was given for them by Gedalyeh and Ethel; and when Gedalyeh came for us in his truck, my father slipped out the back door. All were gathered when we arrived; the Russian Hordes in full force, Mischa, his girl, and her parents, whom the Chilesheans had already sized up as *cuptsonim*. Lisping, Mischa made a speech in English which was applauded, and presented Bessie with a ring.

A few months later, when he fell in love with a girl called Sylvia, he stopped payments on the diamond ring he had given Bessie, and the jeweller put a garnishee on his wages. Gedalyeh had first knowledge of it and took Mischa to account.

He smacked him in the face, causing his nose to bleed. Half fainting, Mischa begged forgiveness of his older brother, and in justification of his actions said he had found out something about Bessie, something too shameful to talk about.

And Gedalyeh had to let it go at that. Sylvia, we never met. Friday nights at supper Mischa talked about her. An educated girl, a fine girl from a respectable family. Not like the other one . . . . He kept promising he'd bring her one night, but never did. So far no one had met her, not even his brother, Gedalyeh. As his love affair with Sylvia progressed, we saw less and less of Mischa. All of a sudden the affair with Sylvia was over, and Mischa was back Friday nights for supper.

"What happened?" Ma kept asking him. "What happened?"

"Don't speak," Mischa said, and put his head between

his knees to keep the blood from leaving it.

"Whatever it is, thank God you found out in time," said Ma, and Pa had to leave the table to keep from laughing.

His courtship of Flo, the lady whom he finally did marry, was a curious piece of business. For the longest time no one had an inkling of it, as Mischa for once was keeping mum. Once or twice he did bring up the name Flo, the new hat designer his boss had hired.

"An old maid with short fat legs and an ass as wide as Gedalyeh's truck. But a pair of hands? Pure gold."

Again and again we heard how business had picked up one hundred percent since the advent of the new hat designer, Flo. He passed us up one Friday, and the following Friday explained that his boss had asked him to escort Flo to a hatters' showing at the Royal York, with dinner afterwards.

"You should see the way they treated her," he said. "Like a queen. All the big hat manufacturers and the buyers. Who looked at my boss and his wife? Nobody. Only to her they paid attention, big ass and all."

More and more the name Flo cropped up in Mischa's conversation. Except now we were hearing more about her head and less about her behind.

"What a business head. Mmm-mm-mm. My boss wants to take her in for a partner."

Another Friday he telephoned his Auntie Chayele, excusing himself. "Flo wants me to go with her to her parents for supper, and I can't refuse."

"What a house," he reported the following Friday.

"What a table. And the food—don't speak. And a servant handing around things. A very refined family."

Never for a moment did we connect Mischa's admiration of Flo with any romantic interest in her. It was Mottele Blabbermouth who spilled the beans. Mottele Blabbermouth, second cousin to Gedalyeh and Mischa, was a felt operator for the firm where Mischa was now head blocker. It was through him, Mottele, that Mischa had first been taken on and apprenticed to a blocker.

"Wait," he said to Ma, "you'll soon have *nachess* from your nephew. Soon he'll be a hat manufacturer in business for himself."

"Mischa is going in business?" she asked.

"Wait, not so fast," Mottele said. "First he'll have to take the old maid, the hat designer, under the wedding canopy. Then he'll be a hat manufacturer with a partner in the business, in the bed. He's not playing around with no Bessies now, or Sylvias. With madam it will have to be *tochas offem tish*, you should excuse a coarse expression."

"What do you mean under the wedding canopy? They're engaged?"

"It wasn't given out yet they're engaged," Mottele said.

"All I know is she's wearing a ring . . . . But you don't have to put a finger in Mottele's mouth."

"It's a few weeks now since he didn't come for supper," Ma said, reflecting. "But he explained he's working overtime—"

"You betcha," said Mottele Blabbermouth.

A month later it was given out that Mischa *was*

engaged. He had brought Flo to Gedalyeh and Ethel to be introduced, and the next day we had it at firsthand from Gedalyeh.

"A very intelligent woman," he said, "and not so bad looking. She's not exactly a young girl, but Mischa is not exactly a young boy anymore. He's twenty-seven years old. At his age I was married and Ethel was carrying for a second time."

A week to the day and without warning Mischa brought Flo to the house to "become acquainted with his Auntie Chayele." Ma, in an apron sodden wet down the front and her hair dishevelled, was swabbing down the linoleum, pushing the old broom around with a wet rag under it. And her embarrassment?—don't speak. Attempting to get out of her apron, Ma got her fingers so entangled in the knotted strings behind that she was unable to take the white-gloved hand Flo proffered.

Now that Mischa was officially engaged, the Chilesheans began clamouring to meet his future bride. "We'll make a big party in my house," said Haskele the Shikker. "In my front room alone you can put fifty people. I'll pay for the whisky, and between the women if everybody makes something there'll be plenty to eat."

But Mischa knew this would be most impolitic. He knew it would be overwhelming in the extreme for a well-bred lady from a refined home to meet them all in one go, and so in the following weeks they were introduced to Flo in groups of four and five until the whole tribe had been accounted for.

"You must meet my parents," Flo said at one of the soirees; and Bencheh the Bed-Farter was heard to remark, "Her parents are still alive? They must be two hundred years old."

Twice a date was set for the wedding, and twice postponed. The first postponement was occasioned by the death of Flo's only sister. A second date was set up, and Flo's mother died. The wedding was again put off for a year, so Mischa was thirty when he was married, and his bride, it was said, a good forty-two, if not more.

A week before the wedding, Mischa came to us for his last supper as a bachelor. "Uncle," he said to my father, "you will do me a great honour if you come to my wedding. I know you don't like my relations and I can't blame you—"

"You do me a great honour," my father said, becoming as formal as Mischa.

"Oh God," Mischa groaned on leaving, "a lot of Flo's relations are coming from the States. If only for once my *mishpocha* will act like human beings."

We heard that Mischa, on leaving our house, made a call on Haskele the Shikker and spoke privately to Haskele's wife, Fenya.

"Fenya, I want you to keep your husband away from the booze. I don't have to remind you how he fell down dead drunk at Shaindl's wedding? I don't want this to happen at my wedding, please."

"Leave it to me," Fenya said, not at all offended. "He got drunk at Shaindl's because I wasn't there to keep an eye. You don't remember I was sick in bed? But to your wedding he's coming with a policeman. Me."

The following Sunday at a quarter to six, and with the synagogue lit like Fontainebleau, the entire wedding company had been seated. The first arrivals, a carload of Chilesheans numbering eight, rushed the hired ushers and raced down the aisle, grabbing the front seats. They were politely, but firmly, routed and shown to their places in order of family precedence. There were a few asides, mutterings and grumblings—all right, so Chayele has a right to sit in a front seat on the groom's side, and even her husband, the Rumanian Beast, has a right too. But by what system does Tamara the Slop get to sit four benches in front of us?

Six o'clock sharp Mischa came down the aisle. He was in a suit of midnight blue, his face was drained of colour, and with knees sagging looked as if he was being held up by Gedalyeh and Ethel, each of whom had him by an arm. He took his place under the canopy and the next minute Flo came down the aisle, escorted by her father and an aunt from the States. She was wearing a hat of her own design and a smartly tailored pearl-grey suit. She took her place beside Mischa, and the rabbi began the service.

Flo, in the traditional manner, circled the bridegroom three times; and when the glass was put under the bridegroom's foot, he stamped on it, smashing and splintering it with the first try. Pinnie the Intellectual (and also an amateur actor who had once shaken the hand of Jacob Adler) jumped on a bench, took his pince-nez from the breast pocket of his rented tuxedo, hooked it on his nose, and in his actor's voice called in English, "Let joy be unconfined!"

A rush was made towards bride and groom, and in less time than it takes to tell the bride's face was smeared with lipstick, her hat was askew and the front of her pearl-grey suit stained orange by a popsicle given to one of the kiddies by its mother during the service. (It was later said of Flo that she "took it like a sport.")

The four-piece band in the adjacent hall struck up the lively "*Chossin-Chaleh-Mazeltov*"; and the wedding company, clapping in tune, trooped after bride and groom, who were now arm in arm, to the hall where tables had been set up against walls, with a space cleared centre floor for dancing afterwards. Ma, tightly corseted and looking grand, blushed like a girl when she was applauded at being seated in a place of honour to the left of the groom, her husband beside her.

The company then was seated in groups of eight, a bottle of whisky at each table. Right away Haskele the Shikker reached for the bottle. Fenya grabbed it away from him.

"I'm in charge here," she said, and passing over Haskele's glass she poured everyone, including herself, a shot of whisky, then put the bottle on the floor between her feet.

"I don't even get to drink *l'chaim* to the couple?" Haskele protested.

"With water," Fenya said. "I see how people which they have weak stomachs drink *l'chaim* with a glass of water.

And people which they have weak heads should do the same."

Waiters came to table with the first course, gefilte fish. Again Pinnie the Intellectual jumped from his place. This time he took centre stage. "*Chevreh*," he called, flinging his arms wide. "Stop! We will not consume a mouthful of food till the couple dances a waltz." He turned to the leader of the four-piece band (a group which Pinnie through his connections with out-of-work musicians had assembled) and made him a deep bow.

"Maestro, if you please, the 'Sweetheart Waltz.'"

The couple smiled and shook their heads, but Pinnie had started a round of applause, and willy-nilly Mischa and Flo took centre floor and waltzed to the strains of "Let Me Call You Sweetheart I'm In Love With You," the vocalist of the group singing the lyrics. It was observed by a few ladies that the bride's choice of pearl grey was an unfortunate one. It made her look too wide across the beam.

All through dinner Mischa was on tenterhooks. He hardly put a mouthful of food to his lips. He was expecting any minute now his people would break out, would become coarse, lewd, and cause embarrassment to himself, to Flo and to the relatives from the States, about a dozen well-dressed, well-mannered and well-spoken people. But no, his *mishpocha* was for once acting like human beings. They were noisy, it's true, laughing and calling to each other across tables, but nothing ribald, nothing lewd, nothing to cause embarrassment. And certainly Pinnie the Intellectual, with his pince-nez and tuxedo, was a credit to the groom's side.

When the dancing began, the kiddies got a bit out of hand sliding up and down the floor, bumping into people—but they were not restrained or ordered off the floor. Kiddies, what can you expect? Let them enjoy themselves, soon they'll be tired. And about ten o'clock they did begin to wilt, and some with glazed eyes sat on the floor, their backs against walls, and others like peasants under a cart fell asleep under tables. Raisel the Galloping Consumptive insisted on doing a solo *kazatska*, and the band obliged her with a tune. Kicking up her heels she danced a lively whirling *kazatska*, for which she had a reputation in the old country, and was going great guns till one of her spike heels broke, causing her to take a pratfall. Mischa put a hand over his eyes and groaned, but as Raisel continued in stocking feet to a round of rhythmic applause, chiefly from the American relatives, the groom relaxed and even joined in the applause.

But wait, the evening was not yet over; and Mischa was not yet through with his ordeal. Embarrassment, and of such a nature as to cause him almost to faint, came from the least expected quarter. From Fenya, Haskele the Shikker's wife.

All evening, and as she had promised Mischa she would, Fenya kept policing Haskele. When he attempted to leave the table during the chicken soup with mandel course, Fenya put a restraining hand on him.

"Where are you going?"

"To the toilet," said Haskele. "You want to come with me?"

"Sure," said Fenya, getting up.

And Haskele sat down to his soup. Several times during dinner, beckoned by a wink and a raised glass from another table, he gave Fenya the slip. But she was at his side like a knife. "I'll take that," she said, and before Haskele had a chance at even a sip, she downed it herself. Fenya, who never took more than an ounce of schnapps at any *simcha*, was by half past eleven rolling drunk. Haskele the Shikker, sober as a judge, got her coat from the cloakroom.

"Come, Fenya. Time to go home."

"No, sir," Fenya said, flinging her arm out and almost knocking him back. "Not till I'll make a speech first."

Fenya, short, stocky, deep-chested and moon-faced with fiery red cheeks, clapped her hands for attention. The company now was seated at the "sweet table" drinking Orange Crush, Coca Cola, lemon tea, brandy, and eating cookies, honey cake, strudel and sponge.

"Come to my side, Haskele," she said, and her husband joined her. "Everybody pay attention," her voice boomed out. "No more do I want to hear the name Haskele the Shikker." She turned her blurred eyes on Mischa. "Especially not from you, *chossin*. He's a good man, a good husband and a good friend. So he takes a little drink once in a while, so what's wrong? No more do I want to hear the name Haskele Shikker, do you hear! Because anybody calls him Haskele Shikker insults me too. Me! Fenya! His wife!"

She walloped herself three times on the chest and fell to the floor. She wouldn't let Haskele help her up. She made it herself and lurched to the "sweet table" and grabbed a bottle of brandy. "Drink, Haskele," she said, holding the bottle out to him. "Take a little drink, sweetheart, and let Mischa Liar talk about you afterwards, who cares?"

In a flash Pinnie the Intellectual was at her side.

"A little discretion, Fenya," he said in English.

She pushed him away. "Attend better to your own business. Attend better to what's-her-name, your wife." Fenya pointed an accusing finger at Pinnie's wife, who was sitting at a side table with the vocalist of the band and drinking Orange Crush out of the same bottle.

Pinnie, widowed the year before, had recently married this scandalously flirtatious lady, ten years younger than him. Haskele clapped a hand over Fenya's mouth and apologized to Pinnie. "Excuse her," he said. "That's what happens to people which are not accustomed to take a drink."

Mischa rose, his face as white as his white-on-white shirt. "What's the matter with her? Is she crazy or something?" He sat down quickly and put his head between his knees. Gedalyeh gave him a sip of brandy.

Shortly after taking the old maid, the hat designer, under the wedding canopy, and as Mottele Blabbermouth had predicted, Mischa was a hat manufacturer in business for himself. With Flo designing hats and dealing with buyers, the business prospered and in no time they were living in a house Up the Hill (north of Eglinton) with wall-to-wall broadloom, a maid and a big car in the garage.

The Chilesheans sniggered. "It's uphill work Up the Hill. Mischa is earning every kopeck, don't worry."

But over the years their attitude towards her changed. She was friendly, she socialized with them—and what's more to the point, the women got their hats at wholesale prices.

Ma, for some reason, never cottoned to Flo. Maybe because she had not come to Pa's funeral? (My father died six years after they were married.) Maybe because on their way home from the factory when Mischa would sometimes drop in for a brief visit with his Auntie Chayele, Flo stayed in the car? (She had said to someone, and this got back to Ma, that she couldn't bear to come in the house, it depressed her so.) However it was, Ma had little to say in praise of Mischa's wife.

At the time of my father's death, my sister, Bella, was a married woman living with her husband and their four-year old boy in a house of their own. I too was married and away from home. Aaron, a bachelor, continued at home. It was a dreadful time for him. Ma was stricken by Pa's death, she wept day in and day out; nothing was of any solace or comfort to her. She had always been a poor housekeeper, but after Pa died she became neglectful to the point of positive slovenliness. It was an ordeal to come Friday nights for supper. One Friday night when I was sweeping up, I got so cross with her I threw the broom against the wall.

"For God's sake, it's murder to come here for supper, everything's so filthy! Why can't you get a woman once a week to clean up. We pay enough—"

(My father, when he died, left nothing. Between the three of us we kept up payments on the house and provided for her keep.)

Ma, at my outburst, looked at me in dismay. She looked at me as if I were the enemy, the enemy who had come to do her in. She grabbed a kitchen knife from the table, and thrusting it in my hand bared her chest and turned a pair of blazing eyes on me.

"Stab me, stepchild! Stab me and make an end! I know since Pa died I'm a bone in your throat."

She turned on Bella and Aaron. "Stepchildren!" She spat the word out and went to her room.

SHE LIVED TEN YEARS after my father died, eight of them in that rundown, five-room house, that misery of a place on Bellevue Avenue from which she refused to budge. She wouldn't come to me, nor would she go to Bella's; neither of us kept a kosher table or observed the dietary laws. It was hard on Aaron who continued at home, and not fair to keep him in bondage like that—but on the other hand, what was to be done with Ma? To leave her alone in the house was out of the question, and so we convened with the brothers, Gedalyeh and Mischa, and tried to come to some solution.

Mischa, at one of the meetings, said, "The main thing is to get her out of that *therrible* house. But where?" He would gladly ask her to come to them, he knew Flo would love to have her—but what was Ma going to do in a big house like theirs alone by herself all day? "Here at least a neighbour drops in, you kids come Fridays for supper and it gives her something to do, you know what I mean?" Suddenly he had an idea. "You know what would be the

171

best plan? We'll fix up the house a little bit, I'll be glad to pay. Get a hold of a painter and a carpenter and I'll pay the bill. When the house is fixed up a little bit, we'll get a *thenant* to move in and Aaron can move out."

The solution came of its own accord. One Friday when we came for supper we found Mrs. Spector in the kitchen, sweeping up. Dishes had already been washed and the table set. Mrs. Spector, a widowed lady, had for years been living four doors down the street with her son, daughter-in-law and three grandchildren. She was without means and entirely dependent on her son's generosity.

The minute we arrived Ma herded us into the bedroom. She put a finger to her lips. "Ssh! Mrs. Spector had a terrible fight with her daughter-in-law." She pointed to a suitcase on the floor. "She even brought her *peckl* here and asked me out of *rachmoniss* to keep her a few days till she finds a place. Now we'll go in and eat. Treat her with respect."

The following Friday Mrs. Spector was still on hand, and again we were herded into the bedroom. "She tried all week to find a place, but who needs an old woman? Maybe it would not be such a bad idea she should stay here . . . ?"

Mrs. Spector stayed five years with Ma. For five years she resisted, turned a deaf ear to the importunings of her son, her daughter-in-law—and why not? For a change she was being treated like a *mensch*, she said. For a change she had money in her pocket. Ten dollars a week we paid her. She would have stayed the rest of her days with Ma, if she had not been struck down by a heart attack, poor woman.

Mrs. Spector, an avid bingo player, was felled one

night, the night she was trying for the 250-dollar prize at the Knights of Columbus giant bingo game. She was within one number of filling her card, and when someone in the hall called "Bingo!" her heart failed, poor woman!

After Mrs. Spector's demise we got a young couple, an immigrant pair who jumped at the chance of two rooms rent free for doing a general cleanup for Ma, her marketing and putting out the garbage. Before they moved in, we had their rooms painted, the upstairs hall, the downstairs hall and the kitchen. Mischa was so pleased. "You see what a difference a little bit of paint makes?" He had long since forgotten that he said he would be glad to pay. Between the three of us we split the cost.

Ma went so rapidly into a decline after Mrs. Spector's death, it was pitiful. Her hair thinned so you could see through to her scalp. Her eyesight failed and she became hard of hearing. She mourned Mrs. Spector and became frightened now on her own account. A slight cold sent her into a panic. "Am I going to die?" she would ask.

The immigrants were kind to her. They undertook many jobs they had not bargained for—but, oh, how lonely she was without Mrs. Spector in the kitchen chattering away. (The couple worked during the day and five nights a week went to school.)

I would come sometimes during the week and find Ma in the kitchen twirling her thumbs and talking to herself. "A blessing on your head," she'd say. "The day is like a year."

One Friday we found Ma on her knees struggling with

the water pan under the old icebox. She had forgotten to empty it and now it was brim full.

"Let me," said Bella.

Ma ordered her away. "I'm not yet helpless."

She gave the pan a terrific wrench and in a second the kitchen floor was inundated and she was knee deep in water. Slowly she rose, and sopping wet took a chair. My sister and I began mopping up. At that moment Mischa arrived on one of his flying visits.

"What's the matter? What happened?" he asked, skipping out of the way of our sloshing mops.

Ma, by way of answer, took a knife from the table. "I'll kill myself. I'll put a knife to my throat and that will be an end to it."

"Auntie Chayele!" Mischa screamed, and springing forward grabbed the knife from her—a knife that wouldn't cut butter.

He called us into a huddle. "Look," he said, "that old icebox is ridiculous. We'll put in a frig, I'll be glad to pay." Immediately he brought out a memo pad, and assessing the approximate height, width and depth of the old icebox, he scratched some figures on the pad and put it away. "Okay," he said, "I know what size will go in here. I'll order it tomorrow from Eaton's and by Wednesday it'll be here. Don't say anything to her, I want it to be a surprise." He embraced his Auntie Chayele and went home.

We expected nothing to come of this, nor did it.

The immigrants stayed three years; and having saved up enough money to buy a house of their own, gave notice.

174

We advertised in the Jewish paper for a companion-housekeeper, and the only applicant was a hefty, broad-faced woman. But she was pleasant enough—all smiles and grateful for the chance of a "real home."

It was a Monday we hired her, and when we came for supper Friday she was sitting beside Ma, just finishing her own supper.

"She's a darling," she said, and giving Ma a kiss on the cheek went up to her own quarters.

"She seems like a nice woman, do you like her?" we asked Ma.

Ma shrugged. "And if I don't? Am I mistress now in my own home? I'm like a baby now. I'm in your hands, do with me what you like."

"I don't like the looks of that dame," Aaron said after the woman had been with Ma a month. "She's sweet as honey when we're here, but if you ask me anything, I think Ma's scared of her. I think she's bullying her around. The fight's gone out of the old lady, didn't you notice?"

Now that Ma had a companion I had stopped dropping in on her during the week, as I used to do. I decided right then that I'd do a little spot-checking, and the following Tuesday without warning I came to the house. At the door I could hear the woman screaming. Ma was sitting beside the stove, and the woman standing over her was holding a frying pan practically under her nose.

"Look what you did!" she was hollering. "You're blind as a mole, deaf as a post, what do you put a frying pan on the stove! You burned a hole in it. Look!"

The woman started when she saw me, and the next minute was all smiles. "Like a child," she said. "Look what she did."

I grabbed the skillet from her and threw it to the floor. "It's her pan!" I screamed. "She can burn a hole in it if she wants to! Pack up and go. Right this minute."

"Let her burn the house down. See if I care," said the woman.

"It's her house," I screamed, following her halfway upstairs. "And she can burn it down if she wants to—"

I returned to the kitchen and Ma was crying. "Deliver me," she said. "Find a place for me to lay my head."

We found a place for Ma, a small nursing home on Beverley Street with kosher food, decently furnished and adequately staffed. At first she had to share a room with a toothless old lady, a shrivelled wasted little thing, bald as a peeled onion and dotty in the head. She kept a baby doll in bed with her, a naked pink rubber doll the size of an eight-pound baby, and crooned over it and kissed it—and sometimes for being naughty smacked its bottom and flung it out of bed. Then she'd cry for her baby, and Ma would retrieve the rubber doll and put it back in bed with her.

In a week Ma had her own room. She was comfortable and she enjoyed her food. To begin, the brothers Gedalyeh and Mischa came regularly to see her, but after a while slackened off.

"Has Gedalyeh been?" we'd ask her. "Mischa?"

"Oh, yes," she lied, not wanting to shame them. She kept a crumpled bit of paper in her pocket with their

176

telephone numbers, and once in a while would ask a nurse to dial for her. And singly or together the brothers would come hotfooting it to spend a few minutes with her. But after she'd had a stroke Mischa spent hours beside her the two days she lay in an oxygen tent. He wept and he wrung his hands and implored her response.

Now here we were, back from burying Ma: the sorrowing nephews and their wives, and we three, the orphans she had brought up. Gedalyeh's tears, after three whiskies, had subsided; half asleep now he was moaning and rocking from side to side. Mischa, after a second schnapps, had also come to himself. And Flo, as it seemed almost certain now that her husband would weather it without going into a second faint, had left her perch on the arm of his chair. My sister, an immaculate housekeeper, had cleaned up the mess of Kleenex at Gedalyeh's feet and was in the kitchen making a pot of tea.

Now the business at hand had to be settled: the week of mourning. *Shivah.* Gedalyeh, the patriarchal figure of the group, opened the discussion.

"So where are we going to sit *shivah*?"

Aaron, being a bachelor, was exempted without further ado. Gedalyeh turned his red-rimmed eyes in my direction. "By your place?" Almost immediately, and without giving me the chance of a reply, I too was exempted. It had just come to him in his befuddled state that my place would be inappropriate, most unseemly. I was married to a *goy.*

"Excuse me," he said. "I forgot."

My sister, Bella, was given the nod. "By your place,

Bella. Anyway, you're the oldest child."

My sister bridled, she reared. "What gives you the right to appoint my house to sit *shivah*? If you want to sit *shivah*, make it at your house or Mischa's. I couldn't care less about this meaningless, antiquated custom. Besides, you should know by now how my husband would react. (My sister's husband was a Communist.) He wouldn't be found dead in a house of *shivah*—"

At once I was hysterical. I began giggling and couldn't stop. Aaron, his face stretched wide in a smile, poured himself a drink.

Kind-hearted Ethel took over. "I know you kids are of the same mind your father was, God rest him. Free thinkers. But I think at a time like this you have to consider what people will say."

Mischa rose. "There's no use *thalking*, let's go home." At the door he stopped. "I suppose you know in about six or eight months we'll have to put up a stone? Or is this also something you couldn't care less about?"

My sister, still nettled, shrugged.

"Okay, forget it," he said. "I'll look after it myself."

The nephews went home with their wives, and the three orphans got tight.

Six months went by, eight months, and not a word from Mischa. Then almost a year and still no word. Nor had we seen any of the Chilesheans. One night we were talking about Ma lying in an unmarked grave. "Let's do something about it," Bella was saying. "It doesn't have to be anything fancy—"

And by the strangest coincidence, and at that precise moment, Mottele Blabbermouth telephoned.

"How come you didn't come to the unveiling?" he asked of my sister.

"What are you talking about?" she said.

"Chayele's stone was unveiled last Sunday, didn't you know? Mischa Liar put up a big stone, a beauty. Everybody was there except you kids."

"We didn't know," my sister said. "Mischa didn't telephone, nobody told us—"

Mottele whistled. "Son-of-a-gun. The whole *mishpocha* was there. It was like a second funeral. Gedalyeh cried something terrible and Mischa fainted twice and everybody was asking, 'Where's Chayele's kids?' Son-of-a-gun!"

Next day we journeyed out to the cemetery by taxi, and as none of us had any recollection as to the exact location where Ma had been buried the year before, we proceeded to do a reconnaissance, each of us going off in different directions.

Aaron spotted it first. He was standing before a tremendous block of red granite, a tombstone dominating the cemetery, dwarfing every stone around and about it. In gold-leaf lettering the inscription read, SACRED TO THE MEMORY OF OUR BELOVED AUNT CHAYELE.

Immediately my sister was affronted. "Trust Mischa to do something like this. A vulgar, pretentious display. Meaningless. It makes me sick to look at it. Let's get out of here."

The keeper of the cemetery, a bearded old man, came

out of his hut and advanced towards us."*Shalom*. I see you're admiring this stone," he said in Yiddish. "Did you know the person lying here? I never had the privilege to meet her," he went on without waiting for a reply. "But I did have the privilege to meet the nephew, a very fine man who put this stone up to her memory, and I understand from him that she was a poor woman, a widow without children. Many rich people lie here, but look around, you won't find a stone like this in the whole cemetery. *Shalom*," he said and returned to his hut.

Glossary

bik bull

chevreh friends; friendly circle

chossin bridegroom

cuptsonim poor people

Erev Shabbos Friday evening, when the Jewish Sabbath begins

gazlan robber, criminal, racketeer, murderer

goniff thief

goy a Gentile

gutkes long winter underwear

haimisher mensch a good soul; decent person

kaddish Jewish prayer of mourning for the dead; also the son who recites such a prayer for a deceased parent

klog a lament; expression of woe

kurveh slut; whore

landsmen people from same town or region in the Old Country

mensch a human being, behaving in a respectable and dignified way

mishpocha family

Molochamovis angel of death

nachess an overflowing sense of satisfaction and pride

nafka prostitute

peckl package or piece of baggage, perhaps carried on the back

Poshe Yisroel impious Jew; a sinner

rachmoniss compassion

shadchan matchmaker

shamus sexton of a synagogue

shaygets Gentile man

shikker drinker; drunk

shiksa Gentile woman

shivah in Jewish custom, period of mourning after a funeral (usually seven days)

simcha a wedding or similar happy celebration

tochas offem tish a coarse expression meaning "ass off the table"

yarmulke skullcap